ONCE UPON A DECADE:
Tales of the Fifties

Short Stories By:

Clark Zlotchew

Comfort PUBLISHING

Copyright ©2011 by Clark Zlotchew
Library of Congress Control Number: 2009939516

Once Upon a Decade: Tales of the Fifties

All rights reserved. The author guarantees all contents are original and do not infringe upon the legal rights of any other person or work. No part of this book may be used or reproduced, stored in a retrieval system or transmitted in any form or by any means without prior written permission of the publisher, except in the case of brief quotations embodied in critical articles and reviews.

For information, address Comfort Publishing, PO Box 6265, Concord, NC 28027. The views expressed in this book are not necessarily those of the publisher.

First printing

Book cover design by Colin L. Kernes

ISBN: 978-1-935361-18-3
Published by Comfort Publishing, LLC
www.comfortpublishing.com

Printed in the United States of America

Acknowledgements

Some of the short stories contained in this book have been published in magazines, some in English, others in my Spanish versions. One was translated from my Spanish version into Italian, and published in Milan. One story appears on the Internet in English and in Spanish.

In English:

"The Unexamined Life," *The New Review: A National Magazine of Contemporary Literature*, No. 5 (Fall 1993), 53-56.

"Circle Dance," *Tier Drops* (1993), 19-23.

"Getting the Message," *Lake Effects*, 1996, 9-14.

"Shame," *Writers Post Journal*, May 2006.

In Spanish:

"The Smell of Land" Spanish version: "Sin complicaciones," *Foro Literario* (Uruguay), No 13 (primer semestre 1985), pp. 13-18.

"A Time to Reap" Spanish version: "Carpe diem," *Foro Literario* (Uruguay), No. 17 (primer semester 1987), pp. 17-22.

"The Unexamined Life" Spanish version: "Formas de ceguera," *Letras de Buenos Aires* (Argentina), año 7, No. 19 (sept. 1988), pp. 63-70.

"The Unexamined Life" Spanish version: "Formas de ceguera," *Plural: Revista Cultural de Excélsior* (Mexico), 2da época, Vol. XXII-V, No. 208 (enero 1989), pp. 45-48.

"Circle Dance" Spanish version: "Baile circular," *Plural: Revista Cultural de Excélsior* (Mexico) 2da, época, Vol. XXII-V, No. 257 (febrero 1993), pp. 12-14.

"Circle Dance" Spanish version: "Baile circular," *Confluencia: Revista de Cultura y Literatura Hispánica, (Colorado)* Vol. 8, No. 2

and Vol. 9, No. 1 (Spring and Fall 1993), pp. 325-28.

In Italian:

"The Smell of Land," from my Spanish, "Sin complicaciones," trans. into Italian by Franca Meo as: "Senza Complicazioni" *Alla Bottega: Rivista Bimestrale di Cultura ed Arte* (Milan), 27, 2 (March-April 1989), 12-15.

On the Internet

Published In English:

"The Enigma of Reginald Savage" http://badosa.com/n322
June 2009.

Published in Spanish:

"El enigma de Reginald Savage" http://badosa.com/n322-es
July 2009.

Foreword

The narratives in this collection paint a picture of an era etched in the soul of those who lived through the 195Os. It also opens the eyes and the imagination of their children and grandchildren, to whom this lost civilization will appear quaintly alien on the surface, but intensely familiar on a more profound level.

Many of the elements of this culture will repel: racism, sexism and homophobia, for example. Women were often objectified as nothing more than a means of creating pleasure and/or children for a man. Their influence ranged from minimal to zero in business and politics. Racial segregation was strictly enforced in the Deep South. Out of fear, those with same-sex orientation, would do all in their power to hide this fact. These ugly elements are reflected in many of the stories of this collection.

Yet this was an era in which the threat of terrorism did not exist for the average American. The plagues of AIDS, Ebola and SARS were unheard of, and penicillin was the magic elixir that would cure whatever ills presented themselves.

In the fifties there were no computers, faxes, email, video games or CDs. At the opening of this period, television was just beginning to become the indispensable household appliance it is today. People wrote by hand, or with a typewriter, using carbon paper to make copies. A man's expectations for the third date with a woman were, theoretically, for a goodnight kiss. Premarital virginity was of supreme importance, and unwed mothers were relegated to the margins of society. Divorce was stigmatized and comparatively rare.

It was a world in some ways more cruel, more demanding, less forgiving. In other ways it was safer, more secure, more comfortable. However it might be characterized, it certainly was *different* from the present. Yet, our basic nature has remained unchanged since humans became humans. The deepest of needs, beyond basic sustenance –love, sex, respect, self-esteem, power— always lie just below the surface as motivating forces. It is only the physical, political, social and moral strictures --fleeting conditions that channel those primary drives-- that change.

The vanished society of the fifties is the setting for the great majority of the narratives in the present collection. Two of the stories refer to a more recent time. They deal with love and death, with triumphs and defeats, with possible witchcraft and with the tension between ethnicity and assimilation. One takes place against the background of racial segregation in the Deep South, while others present adventure on the high seas as well as a glimpse of Havana night life on the eve of the Castro Revolution.

C. M. Z.

Table of Contents

Acknowledgements

Dedication

Foreword

Witch's Brew...**1**

Ladies' Man...**13**

The Smell of Land...**23**

Wax Apples...**33**

Circle Dance...**39**

Charisma...**43**

Getting the Message...**51**

Initiation...**57**

Persuasion...**61**

Storm Warning...**69**

Shame...**79**

A Time to Reap...**83**

The Enigma of Reginald Savage...**89**

Fear of Failure...**103**

Going for the Gold...**111**

The Unexamined Life...**119**

Nostalgic Journey...**127**

Dedication

Special gratitude to Jessica M. Olson whose sincere admiration and enthusiasm for these stories encouraged me.

To my wife Marilyn for her support and patience.

To Otto Dierkes and Bernard Schraer, who accompanied me through the world of the Fifties.

To Nina Dierkes, for the encouragement of her profound insight into the underlying meaning of these stories.

WITCH'S BREW

We'd been back home on liberty for a few days and were in Tedesco's in Union City when this incredible thing happened. There we were, me and Rhino Mahoney and Danny Andreotti, just trying to have a bite to eat and a good talk. We were minding our own business, sitting around one of those tables in a booth, guzzling our beers and waiting for the waitress to bring the chow. But what she brought wasn't just food.

You see, we all got what we ordered, except for Andreotti. He'd ordered a turkey sandwich on white with lettuce, tomato and mayo. But the waitress got it wrong. She brought him the hot open-faced sandwich with gravy and French fries. So Andreotti told her, nice and polite, you understand, that he ordered the *cold* sandwich. But the waitress said, "No, you didn't. You ordered the *hot* sandwich."

"No, it was the cold sandwich," he told her.

The waitress slammed her fist down on the table, making the beer bottles dance, and yelled, "Hey, give me a break! If I go back and get the cold turkey, and bring them back the hot one, they'll take the hot one out of my pay."

Andreotti raised one eyebrow, like he does, and said, real slow, "Gee, I'm sorry, but I didn't order the hot one, and I don't want it. And I sure as hell don't want to pay for it."

She said, "Look, you think that just because you're a good-looking guy you can do whatever you want?"

We were all watching and listening, and we couldn't believe this conversation. I guess Andreotti thought she was getting too personal. He said, "C'mon, I'm not doing whatever I want. I just want the sandwich I ordered."

So, then, she laid the plate down, leaned over him real close, her face no more than six inches from his, and said, "Look. Either you take the hot turkey sandwich like a good boy, or I'll put a curse on you."

So help me, she said she was going to put a curse on him! Then she kind of thought about it for a minute, looked from one to the other of us, and said, "Better yet, I'll put a curse on the three of you."

Well, the three of us just looked at each other. We didn't know whether to laugh or get mad. I mean, whoever heard of putting a curse on someone in Union City, New Jersey, in this day and age? It was crazy!

I took a good look at her. She was about 40 or so, dark-haired, hawk-nosed, piercing eyes...not bad looking, in a worn-out sort of way. But her eyes had purplish shadows under them, at least that was the way they looked in the restaurant. Maybe it was the lighting.

And it's funny, but she reminded me of Andreotti's mother-the way she looked when we were eight years old, not long before she died. His mom was always yelling at him to eat more, because he was a skinny kid. She had always been after him to finish everything on his plate, which he never did, of course. And she used to say how he was driving her to her grave 'cause he wouldn't finish his food.

And he used to crack, "Well, you don't want to *walk* there, do you, Mom?"

Anyhow, the waitress looked at Andreotti and said, "So, what's it gonna be: hot turkey with gravy or cold turkey with the *malook*?" And she just stood there looking at him, as if she'd said something ordinary, as if she'd asked Andreotti a reasonable, everyday kind of question, like, 'What kind of dressing do you want on your salad?' and was calmly waiting for an answer.

"Look," he said, "just get me my cold turkey, okay?" He sounded annoyed. Hell, he *was* annoyed, naturally.

Then she straightened up, stared a hole through his face and shot back, "You want cold turkey, you're gonna get cold turkey, buster. Plus the *malook*!" And she went back to the kitchen.

"What the hell's a *malook*?" asked Rhino.

"You know," Andreotti said, "*mal'occhio*, the evil eye. It's Italian."

Then the waitress came back, dumped the plate with the cold turkey sandwich on the table and said, "From now on, you guys are going to suffer. You," she said, looking right at Andreotti, "are going to be losing your temper all the time. You won't be able to control it and it's going to cost you. Believe me, it's going to cost you. It's going to mess you up real good. It's going to drag you down to the bottom of hell."

Then she looked around the table at the rest of us and said, "And you're such good friends of his, eh? Well, he'll drag you down along with him." She smiled and nodded her head a couple of times, as if she were saying, "Just you wait and see." Then she added, "Lots of luck, guys. Enjoy your dinner."

Now, by this time, we weren't feeling too hungry anymore. I know *I* wasn't. And the other guys looked like I felt. Well, we got through the meal, but we didn't really enjoy it. The conversation wasn't what you'd you call too great, either, as you could guess. I mean, she really put a damper on the whole evening. Now, that's not to say that any of us believed in curses, not in this day and age. We weren't superstitious, but, at the same time, who knew? Anyhow, it was not exactly relaxing to have your meal served by someone who *thought* she was putting a curse on you or, when you come right down to it, who even *wanted* to do that to you. Well, we got the hell out of there as soon as we finished eating, instead of hanging around and chewing the fat some more, like we always used to do.

There was a problem to take care of before we got out of there: the tip. Now, it isn't customary to tip someone for giving you rotten service, plus a *malook* for dessert, right? Right. But...the thing was, just on the outside chance that she actually *could* give us the evil eye, we wouldn't want to chance not giving her anything at all, either, you know? Because, then she might make it even worse...that is, if she really could do anything at all, of course.

Now, nobody wanted to act as if they believed she was serious, yet nobody wanted to push her any further. So, after a lot of arguing back and forth about the tip, we left her exactly ten percent of the bill, before tax. I thought maybe we ought to go and talk to old man Tedesco himself, if he was there, or whoever was running the place, but Rhino said we should drop it and just leave. When I thought about it, I agreed with Rhino. I figured Andreotti gave her enough grief already, even though it really wasn't his fault. Besides, she probably wasn't playing with a full deck.

"This is weird," I said. "Here we are, in a nice neighborhood restaurant on Bergenline Avenue in the middle of the 20th century. You can see the lights of New York City right there across the Hudson, plain as day. The Big Apple, U.S.A., capital of the modern world, and look at us," I said, "we're worrying about some crazy curse."

Andreotti raised an eyebrow, like he does, and said, "Who's worrying? Nobody's worrying."

So then I said, "Then, what's the hurry?"

∞ ∞ ∞

Andreotti and I were down in Savannah about a month later. Before we went ashore on liberty, Chief Barker gave us a speech about getting into fights with the locals – or, rather, about *not* getting into fights. First, he looked around to see if everyone was paying attention, and then he began to talk.

"You boys are about to go on liberty, and I'm sure a lot of you are going to want some liquid refreshment." He looked around to see if we knew what he meant. I guess he saw some blank faces, so he added, "That means you're probably going to find yourselves in some bar having a drink - of the alcoholic persuasion, that is. Who knows, maybe even *two* drinks..." He paused for a minute, got the polite laughs he was looking for and went on.

"Well," he said, "sometimes drinks don't mix too well with strangers, especially if you're a Northerner and the strangers are Southerners. I mean, there's a tendency to get into fights under those circumstances." He paused, put on this kind of angelic face and added, "At least that's what they *tell* me." Everybody laughed, because you got the feeling he was talking from sad experience but was trying to sound innocent. Then he put on a real serious face and said, "Now, men, I want to give you some good advice."

He stopped again and looked around at everyone to make sure we were listening. I guess he thought the suspense would make us pay more attention. Then he said, pronouncing each word separately, "Do *not*, I repeat, do *not*, get into any fights. You got that? Just *don't*. Do everything you can to stay out of trouble. You may be a pretty strong guy, you might know how to take care of yourself in a scrap, but, remember, no matter how strong a man may be, no matter how good a scrapper, there's always someone who's just a little stronger, someone who knows how to fight just a little better."

"Besides," he told us, "that's not the point. The thing of it is, you boys are the strangers, the outsiders, here in Savannah. You don't belong here. I don't belong here. The local boys live here. It's their town, and you can't fight a whole *town*. Nobody can, no matter how much of a man you think you are. Or at least you can't fight a whole town and *win*, or even get away in one piece. Besides, the local police are not exactly going to take your side over the local boys'."

Chief Barker stopped talking for a minute and looked around the compartment to see if we were paying attention, I guess, to see if he was making an impression on us. Then he went on.

"Some guy makes a crack in a bar," he said, "about you, about the Navy, about Northerners, whatever. Forget it. Ignore him. Don't even answer him. I know it's hard, but remember, you're never gonna see that guy again. You don't live here, but he does, so what happens here is more important to him than to you, because all his buddies and all his neighbors will remember what happened.

"And if the local boy gets into a fight, he knows he better look good. But, besides that, you get into a scrap with him, his buddies are gonna be there and they're gonna be all over you. And they're gonna win. Believe me, it's their town and there's more of them than there are of you and your buddies. So, just take it easy and turn the other cheek, like it says in the Good Book."

When he said this, the chief put on a look kind of like he was *holy* or something, like a saint. You'd have thought he had a halo. And it seemed really strange on him, with his big beer belly sticking out, holding a mug of coffee in his hand, scratching his balls and always using foul language. But that look of holiness only lasted a couple of seconds.

Right then, I should've realized that I was going to have problems. I was going ashore with good old Andreotti, who was a pretty nice guy, kind of quiet, minded his own business and all, but who had a stubborn streak and sometimes got a little crazy.

One thing about Andreotti: he had a terrific imagination. I mean, he could dream up all kinds of schemes for having fun. However, there's a down side to having too much imagination. Back in high school, in health class, every time we'd be talking about some disease-tuberculosis, meningitis, even *syphilis*, for Christ sake–even though he'd never been with a woman back then, he would think he had the symptoms and would break into a cold sweat about it for a while and couldn't concentrate.

Now, Andreotti wasn't a very big guy. He was about five feet eight inches tall, and weighed about 150 pounds. Compact, you know what I mean? And he was like a volcano. He was quiet and easygoing most of the time, but when the pressure really built up, look out. And, ever since the time that waitress put a curse on him – on *us* - back in New Jersey, Andreotti had been acting peculiar. I mean, he was getting to be more stubborn than usual, even a little crazier than usual. Just a little more each time, so you could hardly notice it, but he definitely was changing for the worse. It was taking less and less pressure to set him off. His volcano was erupting more and more often. It worried me.

Now, while the chief was giving this speech, Andreotti made these little comments under his breath. Like when the chief said, "Now, men, I want to give you some good advice," Andreotti whispered, "It's about time." Or when the chief said, "There's always someone who knows how to fight just a little better," Andreotti muttered, "No shit. That's what it's all about, ain't it?"

Then, when the chief was talking about how the local man's friends and neighbors would remember what happened, so that the local had to look good, Andreotti raised one eyebrow, like he does, and grumbled, "What about *our* feelings? Don't we have to look in the mirror when we shave?" And when the chief mentioned turning the other cheek, Andreotti gave a nasty little laugh and under his breath said, "He means *kiss* the other cheek."

The chief must've heard something, because he asked, "What's that you said, Andreotti?"

Andreotti put on this sincere look and told him, "I said I gotta take a leak, chief."

This definitely was not like Andreotti, not like the Andreotti I used to know. One thing, he had always been level-headed, and would take good advice seriously, not make fun of it. So I should've *known* how things were going to be on liberty. Hell, I guess I *did* know, but what could I do? He was my buddy.

∞ ∞ ∞

We had been walking around, seeing the sights, ogling the girls, trying to pick up a couple of them, when we got thirsty. We were standing at a bar, Andreotti and me. There wasn't any air-conditioning, but the drinks were cheap. Four local guys were playing pool. They were in their late teens and early 20s, wearing jeans and t-shirts, the sleeves rolled up to their shoulders. Some of them had tattoos on their arms, you know the kind. Once in a while, they'd look over at us. They looked like they were making some cracks about us, but we couldn't hear what they were saying.

Further down the bar was a couple of old geezers in carpenter's overalls, and some guy in his late 20s who looked like a bodybuilder. He had a real close crew cut, so close you couldn't tell if his hair was blonde or brown. He kept looking from us to the guys playing pool to the tattoo of the Confederate flag on his right bicep, which he flexed every time he looked at it.

The overhead fans were slowly wafting the cigarette smoke around the room. The place was full of flies buzzing through the air or walking along the bar, eating crumbs of hardboiled egg or saltine crackers. There were coils of fly paper hanging from the ceiling, dead flies stuck to them like raisins on a fruit cake. Damn place smelled like a locker room.

The bodybuilder turned to face the pool players, his elbows propping him up against the bar behind him. He called out, slow and sarcastic-like, "Looks like we got us some company, boys, now don't it?"

One of the pool players spat on the floor. The others gave us a blank stare. Andreotti pushed back his black hair and muttered into his beer, kind of disgusted-like, "Shit!"

The bodybuilder flexed his right bicep, inspected it carefully and felt it with his left hand. Still looking at his muscle, he said, nice and easy, "What's that you said, boy?"

Andreotti looked over at the muscleman, kind of wondering if he really was talking to him. The weightlifter finally looked at Andreotti and said, "Yeah, you, little man. What was that you said?"

"He didn't say anything," I told him. "He was just swishing his beer around in his mouth, is all."

"I wasn't talking to *you*," the gorilla said. "I was talking to the little fellow next to you. And I could swear I heard a nasty word." He looked directly at Andreotti and said, "Didn't you say *shit*, boy? Hey, I'm talking to you!"

I just knew Andreotti wasn't going to be able to say *no*, to calm things down. And, sure as hell, he said, "Yeah, I said *shit*."

"Well, you said a mouthful, boy!"

The retards at the pool table stood there, blank-faced, just watching the whole thing. But when the gorilla started to laugh at his own joke, they all started to laugh too. I got the feeling they didn't know what the hell they were laughing about.

The bodybuilder suddenly stopped laughing, and so did the pool players, except for one, who got an elbow in the ribs from one of his buddies as a signal to get serious. Then King Kong looked over at us, and said, "But seriously, boys, don't y'all know it's not nice to talk like that in a respectable place like this here?"

Seeing that we just kept sipping our beers, he said, "Don't they teach you boys any manners up North?" Then he called over to the pool players, "I wonder who asked these boys in. Hey, which one of y'all invited our guests? Was it you, Billy Joe?"

"Shit, no, Arjay! You kidding?" Billy Joe sounded pissed off, but like it was because Arjay expected him to be. Arjay turned to look at us for about ten full seconds, like we were a pile of manure rotting in the sun, giving off a real strong smell. Then he turned back to Billy Joe, "I didn't think so."

Arjay looked back at us and said, "Hey, y'all – you boys with the pretty white suits and the fancy blue scarves – what the hell you doin' here, anyhow?"

No one answered him. We were ignoring him, but that was getting harder to do. It was hard enough to keep up our own conversation. I was remembering the chief's lecture about not getting into fights with the locals. I guess we both were. I was thinking maybe we should just get the hell out of this bar, but I didn't want to be the one to say so. Andreotti didn't want to be the one to say so either, I guess.

"Hey, y'all..." Arjay yelled to us, "I'm talking to you boys." The pool players were still standing around, holding their cues, watching the show.

"Well, now," Arjay drawled," I guess they just don't want to talk to me. That's not very friendly-like, now is it?"

Arjay folded his arms across his chest, leaned his back against the bar, and looked at us and the pool players at the same time. "Hey, y'all, is it true what they say about damn Yankees...especially if they're Navy boys?" He winked over at Billy Joe and the others.

I noticed the pool players moving closer. The bartender seemed like he'd been enjoying the show, but was starting to look a little worried. I was thinking he was probably worried about having his property trashed, and that made me worry about having *my* property trashed – my most important property - my body.

"Hey," Arjay said, "it's not sociable when you don't want to talk to people, you know? Now, I asked y'all a question. Is it true what they say about damn Yankees, especially sailors?" He put on this big, toothy smile, looked around the room and then back to us. "You know, that they're all queer?"

We had just finished our beers and were about to shove off, but that last remark was just too much for Andreotti, damn his ass. The son-of-a-bitch went and grabbed himself by the crotch and said, "Bite this, asshole."

Shit! We were almost out of there when the crazy bastard had to go and shoot his mouth off. He just *had* to go and do it! The bartender's eyes widened and he looked from Andreotti to Arjay. I looked at Arjay and at the four stooges who were starting to move in. Arjay could have taken the both of us apart without even working up a sweat, and without the help of his pool-playing buddies and their cue sticks. Hell, he could have massacred the pool players *and* the two of us, easily. I wondered if they had laws down there against killing outsiders, unarmed members of the Armed Forces. I wondered if a local jury would ever convict Arjay...I wasn't feeling too comfortable.

Arjay broke into a smile, showing lots of teeth. "Well, now, they *do* know how to talk. Would y'all look at that? Now, what did you just say to me, Missy?"

The bartender whined, "Hey, Arjay, take it outside, will you?"

The pool players were moving in closer, holding their cues, squinting through the cigarette smoke at us.

"Nothing," I said. "He didn't say anything. We were just leaving."

The pool players were now blocking the door.

"No, no...now, he *said* something," Arjay said, ambling toward us. "He surely did say *something*, didn't you, little girl?"

Andreotti's eyes were blazing. His face turned white, then red.

"Forget it, Andreotti," I heard myself saying. "Let's get the hell out of this dump."

The bodybuilder grabbed Andreotti by the arm. "Hey, little

girl, how's about a kiss? Or maybe it's you that wants to do a little biting?"

In one motion, Andreotti picked up his beer bottle by the neck, smashed it against the bar and lunged for Arjay's face. Before anyone else could react, the blow peeled back a flap of flesh, opening a kind of trench. I thought I saw cheekbone before the red began to flow.

Arjay must have been stunned, because he was still smiling when the blood rose to the surface of the wide gash between his nose and his ear. Then, realizing what had happened, his eyes widened in pain and his face went pale. He swung his fist wildly at Andreotti's head, but Andreotti ducked and put his own fist into Arjay's midsection, hard. When Arjay doubled over, Andreotti chopped at the back of his neck and Arjay hit the deck.

Billy Joe and the others blocking the door were frozen with shock for a couple of seconds. I figured I had to do something to clear the way for an escape, so I booted Billy Joe in the groin as hard as I could, the way you'd kick a football. He folded and went down, doubled up and gasping. I grabbed his cue stick, cracked one of the others in the skull with it, sending him to the floor and started swinging it to keep the other two at bay. They backed away from the door. Out of the corner of my eye, I saw that the bartender had a club in his hand. He looked as though he was deciding whether to use it or not.

"Let's get the hell out of here, Andreotti!" I yelled. But the son-of-a-bitch had tasted blood and wouldn't stop. Arjay's face was already a bloody mess, but Andreotti kicked him right in the mouth. I saw teeth and blood splatter onto the floor. The bartender raised his club, leaning over the bar to bash Andreotti's skull. I couldn't blame him, but I couldn't let it happen either, so I came down on the bartender's wrist with the pool cue as if I was chopping wood. He howled, dropped the club and ran into the back room, holding his right wrist with his left hand. I didn't know if he was going to call the police, get a shotgun or what.

"Come on, damn you to hell, let's go!" I yelled to Andreotti. He looked away from the mess that was Arjay. It was as though Andreotti was snapping out of a dream or a spell and was coming back to the real world. I mean, he finally realized we had to get out of there, fast.

One of the two pool players still standing made as though he was going to charge us with the pool cue he held like a baseball bat, but I jabbed him in the gut first with mine and we got the hell out of there. We ran down the street, and as we turned the corner, we heard the bartender yelling for the police and the Shore Patrol.

We made it back to the main drag, blending into the crowd with all those other Navy men, walking slowly, gawking into store windows, checking out the women, trying to look natural. Andreotti actually managed to look natural, except he had this tight little smile on his face. It was only a half-smile, really, just on the left side of his mouth, like he wasn't giving himself permission to fully smile until we were out of danger. I don't know how *I* looked; I just know I felt real shook up.

We started to see more Shore Patrol than usual, and they and the police seemed to be looking at every sailor on the street.

"Should we head back to the ship?" I asked.

"Hell, no. They'll be expecting that. We'll go back tonight at the last minute. It'll look more innocent."

Ironically, despite all the violence, we didn't have a mark on us, but they probably described us as a tall, thin, light-haired man and a short, medium-built, dark-haired man. Andreotti thought of this and said we'd better join up with some of our shipmates so we wouldn't stand out. He sure had a cool head. Well, it was cool *now*, anyway.

We got together with four other guys from our ship and we all headed to a good steakhouse we'd heard about, on a palm-lined road called Victory Drive. We had to hoof it a few miles out from downtown to get there. Our waitress was a real cute blonde, about 19 or 20, I'd say. She talked real sweet, like they all did down there. I mean, she'd take your order by cooing something like, "What y'all goin' have, honey?" And we were all kidding around with her, kind of flirting, you know, and she would smile or laugh and say things like, "Oh, you *are* a *caution*, darlin'" or "Oh, now, be*have* yourself, y'all."

Well, nothing special happened to the rest of us, but it was real weird what happened to Andreotti. It was bad, really bad, but I'm coming to that. He had ordered a steak, with French fries, black-eyed peas and coleslaw. And when she'd asked him how he wanted his steak, he smiled and said, "Very rare. I want to see it jump when I put a fork in it."

When the waitress brought Andreotti the steak, it was so well done that even *I* noticed it. The outside was practically black, and when he cut into it, there was no pink. It was all dark brown. The guys even commented on it. One of them said, "Hell, he wants to see it jump…? It looks like it ought to be buried at sea." Someone else said it looked like you could resole your shoes with it. Everyone was laughing, but Andreotti just stared at it for the longest time without moving a muscle, as though he was lost in thought, or hypnotized or something. He was holding his knife and fork on the steak where he had cut into it, and I could see his hands trembling.

The waitress came over and asked us if everything was all right, and everyone looked over at Andreotti, as though they were waiting for him to say something. The cute little waitress looked over at him, too, but he just kept staring at his plate. This was not like Andreotti. I mean, he'd usually take every opportunity he could to kid around with a good-looking girl. Something was wrong, really wrong.

The waitress looked worried, and went over to Andreotti now. She said, "Isn't your steak the way you wanted it, darlin'?" She said it in the sweetest way, but he didn't answer. Some of the other guys told her he had really wanted it very rare. "Remember," one of them said, "he wanted to see it jump."

The waitress turned red, bit her lip and said, "Oh, I'm *so* sorry, sir. Y'all must think I'm real dumb. Here, let me take it back for you, honey."

She tried to take the plate, but Andreotti grabbed it with both hands and wouldn't let her pick it up. "No," he said. "It's okay. Just leave it."

"But, sir, it's no trouble…"

"Just leave it!" He was practically screaming.

The waitress took her hand off the plate as though it was white-hot. She looked scared. We were all staring at Andreotti, but nobody said anything. He looked up at us and saw us gaping at him. He looked at the waitress and saw she was frightened. He took her hand gently and, I swear to God, there were tears in his eyes. When he spoke, his voice was kind of shaky.

"It's okay, sweety. It's okay, really. I like my steak this way. You just watch, I'm going to finish it. You'll see. I'm going to eat every last bit of it. There won't be anything to throw away. You'll be proud of me."

So help me, I thought I heard him say *Mom* after he said she'd be proud of him. That was weird: *Mom*… Now, I'm not 100 percent sure, but I think that's what I heard. Then he slid off his chair and got down on his knees - on his goddamn *knees*, for Christ's sake! - pressed his teary face against the waitress' apron and said, "Don't be mad at me, don't be mad, please."

Andreotti was sort of sobbing. I tell you, it scared the hell out of me. I didn't know what to think, and the waitress just froze at first. Then she patted him on the head, kind of smoothing his hair while the whole damn restaurant stared.

I go to visit Andreotti at the Veteran's Hospital on Long Island whenever I'm in port, but he doesn't talk to me. He just sits there and listens. Maybe he doesn't even do that, I don't know. He's been there about 14 months, and they tell me he's getting better. He'll be all right pretty soon. That's what they say.

LADIES' MAN

When is she going to come?

It's been getting dark earlier. It's October, and the bitter smell of burning leaves makes me want to gag. The leaves on the trees in the park across the street are turning red and yellow, but not all of them. I usually like the fall, but now it makes me feel strange, like everything's hanging by a thread and about to crash down. I'm glad there are still some green leaves left.

Here I am, walking back and forth between Winfield and Bartholdi since school let out. It'll be dinnertime pretty soon, and I'll have to go in and maybe miss her, and the green leaves will turn brown...

What's taking her so long?

Gotta seem nonchalant, hands in my pockets, looking up at the sky or into the windows of the Winfield Pharmacy and of the Sweet Treat Candy Store, as if I really cared what goes on in those places. Big plate-glass window, big black letters: WINFIELD PHARMACY. Past the letters, a huge bottle of green liquid on the left and a huge bottle of red liquid on the right. Between them, a life-sized, full-color photograph of a pretty girl in a red bathing suit smoking some brand of cigarette. Inside, there are people eating ice cream sundaes or tuna sandwiches, and the pharmacist is counting out pills. Me, looking at my own reflection in the glass looking back at me – sandy hair, pimply face, skinny arms – how would I look with the pimples gone, with lots of big muscles? One day, one day...gotta wash my face more often, more carefully. Gotta start lifting weights. What am I looking at my reflection for? What am I looking at the people in Winfield Pharmacy for, and the girl in the bathing suit, smoking a cigarette, the pharmacist counting pills, the bottles of green and red liquids?

They're right there in front of me and I see them, but I don't really see them. I see them with my eyes, but not with my brain, my heart. They're not registering. They're there, but they're not there, not here in my head. I keep seeing *her*. Helen's not here, but I keep seeing her in my mind's eye, in my heart's eye. I see her because I want to see her, because I like seeing her, looking at her...If I keep wanting to see her strongly enough, she'll be here, she'll come. She'll feel that I'm looking at her, that I want her to come, and she'll understand and she'll come. I see her just as plain as I see her in Latin class, as I see her when she is actually there in the flesh, the gorgeous flesh, in Latin class...

Latin class at Snyder High: white-haired Miss Hanley shows us colored prints of stern Roman senators in togas, photographs of the Colosseum, and makes us all drone the declensions of nouns and the conjugations of verbs: *amo, amas, amat, amamus, amatis, amant*...I look longingly at Helen's dark eyes, olive skin and long chestnut hair in Latin class, in the plate-glass window that says WINFIELD PHARMACY, in my mind's eye, and I repeat *amo, amas.*

I never really managed to say anything to her, to speak to her outside of class. I tried twice, but I couldn't do it. One time...*We both arrive at the classroom door at the same time, coming from opposite directions. I see her coming; I try desperately to think of something interesting to say. She smiles, says "Hi" and pauses for the briefest moment, as though she were expecting me to answer, to say something. My heart is pounding wildly. I have trouble breathing. I'm practically panting. Does she notice? My thoughts scatter in all directions, can't hold them together. I feel a fleeting tickling sensation arise in the pit of my stomach and, quick as lightning, fly to my throat. She shrugs and goes into the classroom. God! Why couldn't I say something? Something funny, something interesting...anything. Why do I keep seeing that disaster over and over and over in my head.?*

That other time...

We're leaving Latin class. She drops her books. Should I go over and pick them up for her? She's only 15 feet away. I want to go, but I feel funny, embarrassed. She'll think I'm not as good as she is if I go around picking up her things for her, like some kind of servant. I want to pick the books up for her, I want to help her, do things for her, but she'll make fun of me, look down on me. I'll feel shame, more shame than I do now. She's looking at me. She thinks I ought to go over and pick up her books. She thinks it's only right that I do that. It's the gentlemanly thing to do. Okay, okay. I'll do it.

I run to pick up the books for her and trip over someone's foot. Shit! There goes Jeff now. The dumb jock...he doesn't think about whether he should do something or not; he just goes over and does it. He's lucky. I wish I were like that. But he's a dumb jock. Yet he's happy, isn't he? He's handing her the books. No big deal for him, he's smiling. My God, what guts he has! He not only picks up her books and hands them to her, but then he laughs and calls her *butterfingers*. And she doesn't even get mad, damn her. She just laughs too, damn her to hell! And Jeff even squeezed her shoulder when he called her *butterfingers*. The bastard! And Helen didn't get mad. She just laughed, looking like she was having a good time. Now she's looking at me here on the floor. I start to get to my feet, feeling like a complete idiot.

She puts her hand on her hip and says, "Well, Eddie, I guess you really fell for me, didn't you?" And she laughs. Why is she laughing? Is she making fun of me? My face feels hot as fire. The tickling in my stomach is more like a churning, burning sensation now. She's looking at me like she expects me to answer her, to say something. She has that superior smile on her face. She wants to see how I get out of this. I won't give her the satisfaction. I glance at her - without smiling - for just a fraction of a second. Then I look away. I'm no clown to be laughed at. She was smiling at me, but now she frowns, turns her nose up, does an about-face and marches away.

Maybe she wasn't making fun of me. Maybe she was just fooling around, having fun – not at my expense, but having fun, *trying* to have fun, *with* me, laughing *with* me, not *at* me. Yeah, that could be. I think it was. Oh, I can't stand it! Why did I have to act that way? Why did I have to ruin things? I can't stop thinking about it. I want to kick my stupid cowardly ass around the block. She doesn't even look at me anymore. I feel like I have a rock in my stomach, a boulder. She looks the other way if she sees me, looks the other way, closes her eyes and turns up her nose – her beautiful, sweet, pretty little nose that I want to kiss.

How can I make things right with her? What can I do or say now to make things right? The people are still stuffing their mouths with ice cream sundaes – stuffing their mouths, happy, self-satisfied. Why can't I be like them? Why can't I be happy, satisfied, enjoying myself? They don't know what's it like. They don't know Helen.

The girl in the red bathing suit...she's smoking that dumb cigarette and looking straight at me. Of course, she's *supposed* to look at me. They design them that way, to look directly at the prospective customers, to make us want to buy cigarettes –*their* cigarettes, anyway. Well, not me. No sir. Can't fool me. I'm not going to buy cigarettes just because you're looking at me, baby. And just because you're so good-looking doesn't mean people are going to do whatever you say. No, not me. Anyway, you're not as beautiful as Helen.

Helen...Could I just walk up to her and say, "You're right. I guess I did fall for you?" No. Impossible. I'd die of shame. Even if I said it the way she asked me if I'd fallen for her, like a joke. Not even as if I were joking. It would be too hard. I'd feel that damned tickling in my stomach, my heart would beat like it was going to fly out of my chest, my tongue would stick to the roof of my mouth. I'd probably even pass out with emotion, maybe even die. And everyone would see. It would be too embarrassing, shameful. I've got to suffer in silence, watch her, "worship her from afar," as it says in something we read in English class. Looking at her full lips, her rounded arms, her long eyelashes, her breasts...

God, how I hate myself for being such a coward.

I can't talk to her. Hell, I can't even talk to *anyone* when she's around! Maybe I could *do* something, something physical, to show how I feel – something to make *her* feel something for *me*. Maybe I could risk my life to save hers...

∞ ∞ ∞

The door of Miss Hanley's Latin class opens and a man with a sinister moustache and a wild look in his eye bursts into the class. Furiously, he glances around the room, his burning glare alighting on Helen. The man takes a long knife from under his jacket and marches straight toward her. She protects her face with her crossed arms and screams, "Help me! Oh, help me, someone!"

Everyone is paralyzed with fear, everyone but me. I jump to my feet. I might die if I attempt to save her, but I don't care. I'd rather die trying to save Helen's life than to see her murdered before my eyes. I would not want to live in a world without Helen, knowing that I did nothing to save her life.

So, using the knowledge of judo I got from that Marine booklet, I attack the sinister character, who towers over me with his bulging muscles. It's a fierce battle, but I'm more skillful. I force the knife out of his hand, knock him unconscious with a chop to the back of the neck and tie his hands behind him with my belt. The police arrive and the entire class looks at me with new respect, with admiration and awe.

Helen keeps thanking me, hugging me, kissing me, telling me how brave I am. She tells me she owes me everything. She looks at me with love and admiration in her deep brown eyes. She takes me by the hand to the nurse's office where she insists on washing the long gash on my cheek and dressing the wound with her own gentle hands. She tells me she's sorry, that it looks as though it's so deep that there will be a permanent scar. I tell her it's nothing, and that as long as it doesn't make me repulsive in her eyes, I don't mind, because the scar will remind me of this day, the day she fell in love with me...

∞ ∞ ∞

The catastrophe with the books was two weeks ago. What happened today was worse, much worse, incredibly worse. God,

I can't stand thinking about it. I wish the earth would open and swallow me. I want to disappear from the face of the earth so I won't have to think about it.

Here I am, walking back and forth in front of my house, trying to look like I don't care, like I couldn't care less. And it's hard to do, so hard. I'm sure she'll show up any minute now and apologize for what happened today. She has to. She's just got to. By now she must realize how much it hurt me, even if she didn't realize it back then, when it happened. And she will come, any minute now. *Amo, amas*... Come on, Helen, honey, hurry, it's almost dinnertime, and I'll have to go in and join my folks.

Who's that who just walked into Winfield Pharmacy? I know her. It's Beth Turner. Everyone says she's so good-looking. A lot of the guys think she's really something. I can't see it. Not next to Helen. She is kind of pretty, but not beautiful, not gorgeous like Helen. She's pale-looking, has those watery-blue eyes, those eyelashes you can't even see because they're so light in color – not like Helen with her deep brown eyes and long dark hair and thick black eyelashes... Beth Turner *is* a nice girl, though. She's always friendly and easy to talk to, but so are my friends, and they're guys. Beth just doesn't *have* it, compared to Helen. Nobody has it, compared to Helen.

Beth is eating a hot fudge sundae. I see her through the loop in the big black D of WINFIELD PHARMACY, between the bottle of red liquid and the bottle of green liquid. Actually, she's in the little space between the bottle of red liquid and the picture of the girl in the bathing suit. She takes the long-handled sundae spoon and dips it into the hot fudge, slowly twirls it around so that the fudge sticks to the spoon and doesn't drip too much, then she raises it to her mouth and puts out her tongue to catch the fudge as it starts to drip. She closes her eyes, I guess to lock out everything but the taste of the hot fudge, to get the full pleasure of the taste. Then she licks the spoon clean so as not to miss any of the sticky, sweet fudge clinging to the spoon. She dips the long spoon into the sundae once more, going beyond the fudge surface, deep into the vanilla ice cream below. She brings the spoon, filled with ice cream, to her mouth and purses her lips around it, letting it melt in her mouth, easing it slowly back and forth between her rounded lips, back and forth, back and forth, as it melts in her mouth. She closes her eyes as she does this.

Why doesn't she just go ahead and put the whole damn thing in her mouth and be done with it? Stop playing with it, damn it; just eat it! But, no, of course not, she takes more and slides it back and forth, letting it slowly melt between her lips.

Helen does that with her finger, sometimes, absent-mindedly, I guess. She seems to be in deep thought, listening to Miss Hanley in Latin class. As she concentrates on the Latin, she sort of sucks on her forefinger and slides it back and forth. The tip of her finger is glistening with saliva. I can't stop looking. I can't concentrate on the lesson.

Miss Hanley is asking Helen what the expression, *homo homini lupus est*, means. Somebody in the back of the room snickers, and Helen suddenly pulls her finger from her mouth and looks sullen. She must think they're laughing at her because she doesn't know what the phrase means. Doesn't she know nobody would laugh at her?

Miss Hanley then calls on "Crazy" Charlie, who's been waving his hand wildly. He says, with this big, stupid grin, that it means, "A queer man eats hominy grits on the rollercoaster."

What an idiot! The class is breaking up with laughter. Miss Hanley looks puzzled. She hasn't got a clue. She asks Crazy Charlie how he arrived at that conclusion. Charlie looks around the room, an idiotic smirk on his face, and explains that *homini* obviously means hominy grits, *lupus* is like what we usually call the rollercoaster, the "loop-dee-loop," and that since *est* is German for "he eats," it must be the same in Latin, too, because they're both foreign languages. "And," he adds, with a wink, "we all know what a homo is."

What an idiot.

The class is in hysterics. Miss Hanley is totally confused by his explanation and exasperated with the class's reaction. "Hasn't any one of you studied the assignment? Doesn't any one of you know what *lupus* or *homo* means?" she asks. The poor, clueless teacher, she's completely out of it, totally in the dark.

I know what *homo homini lupus est* means. It means that man is a wolf to man. Man is man's worst enemy and it's a dog-eat-dog world. I'd like to volunteer to give the answer, but I'm not the kind of guy who can call out an answer. If she called on me, okay, I'd give the answer, but I'm not going to stick my neck out. And I don't want to interrupt all the laughing and good feelings of the class by raising my hand to volunteer. But I *do* want Miss Hanley to realize that I had studied and that I know what the expression means, damn it all. I want Helen to see how smart I am too.

Miss Hanley sweeps her gaze around the room and now she's looking at me. But she's not calling on me; she's just looking around the room. How can I show her I know the answer without volunteering and interrupting the laughter? I know, I'll bare my teeth and point with both forefingers to my eyeteeth. This way, Miss Hanley will know I'm subtly signaling the idea of *fangs*, like those of a wolf, and she'll realize I know what the Latin phrase means.

"What on earth are you doing, Edward?" Miss Hanley asks me this as though I were doing something demented and even disgusting, like maybe I was making a puddle on the floor under my desk or had whipped out my peter and was playing with it. What the hell's the matter with the woman? Doesn't she understand that I'm signaling that I know the phrase means *man is a wolf to man*? What is she, senile? Damn her to hell! Everyone is looking at me. I can feel Helen's eyes on me too. My face feels like it's on fire.

"Well, Edward...?"

The stupid bitch! What's she trying to do? Doesn't she realize I'm the only one in the whole, stupid class who knows the answer, the only one who studied the lesson? I can't just sit here until the bell rings. Damn her, she looks like she's willing to just stare at me and wait till hell freezes over for me to explain what I was doing.

Everyone's looking at me. Helen's looking at me. They think I'm crazy or something. I've got to say something, something that shows I'm not crazy. But, whatever I say, I want to sound nonchalant, debonair, like someone who knows what it's all about, not like some kind of bookworm who spends all his time studying. So I kind of mumble, "I'm polishing my fangs."

"You're what...??!!"

Damn that stupid, senile old bitch. Get a hearing aid, why don't you. I tell her, "You know, like a wolf." Then, more quietly I add, "That's what *lupus* means."

"So, you're a wolf, are you?"

From the back of the room, Crazy Charlie calls out, "More likely *homo* than *lupus*."

I want to go back there and bash his nose into his mouth. I hope the ground opens up and swallows me and that clown and that senile fool bitch and the whole freaking class, damn it! Except for Helen. I realize now that my ridiculous fang-polishing pantomime is being taken as a brag that I'm some kind of "wolf," a womanizer. Yeah, I'm a wolf, all right. Everyone knows I can't even talk to a girl, let alone be a wolf.

I wish I were dead.

The bell is ringing. Thank God! I jump out of my seat and run for the door, but Helen is already there. She looks at me with some weird kind of smile, like she's mocking me. Her tone of voice is heavily ironic. "Well, Mr. Wolf," she says, "I'm on my way to Grandmother's house; I guess I better be careful going through the woods." As if that weren't enough, she adds, sarcastically, "I didn't realize you were such a ladies' man, Eddie." Then she closes her eyes that way she does, as if to say she's seen enough of me, turns on her heel and saunters off.

Oh God, oh God, oh God! I can't stand it. Surely, she must realize how much it hurts me to hear her say that. She knows for certain I'm no ladies' man. She has to know that *I* know I'm no ladies' man. Unless, oh God, she thinks I'm such an idiot that I think I actually *am* a ladies' man. She must know I understood she was making fun of me. And, for her, of all people, to make fun of me in that way, about that subject. She *must* understand that I was only trying to show Miss Hanley that I knew what *lupus* meant. By now, she must be sorry for hurting me like that, and she'll surely come down here any minute now to apologize. I'll forgive her, of course. And then I could help her with her Latin conjugations. She needs help, that's for sure. *Amo, amas...* And I'll be happy, so happy. And then...

Beth Turner just noticed that I'm out here looking in. She must think I've been watching her. She doesn't know I'm just staring in without seeing anything, that I'm just standing here thinking about Helen. I see Beth between the huge bottle of red liquid and the bathing suit girl and the huge bottle of green liquid. She's waving her hand at me. She smiles a nice, pleasant smile and motions for me to come in, to come over to her and sit down. She's waving me toward her and points to the seat next to her. That's very nice of her, very friendly, but I want to be out here when Helen comes along and apologizes to me, so I just shrug my shoulders and shake my head at Beth. But I do it with a smile, so she'll know I appreciate her friendliness, but I just can't go inside right now.

She looks annoyed. She shrugs her shoulders, tosses her blonde hair and goes back to working on her hot fudge sundae. She finally finishes it, then stands up, pays the cashier and walks out the door into the street. She walks up to me and kind of hesitatingly asks me why I didn't go inside. I tell her I'm waiting for an important message.

"An important message? What kind of message? From who?"

"It's very important," I tell her, "but I can't talk about it. The government wouldn't like it." I kind of wink confidentially and add, "You know what I mean."

She looks at me like I'm either a raving maniac or I'm putting her on, but she can't decide which.

"Okay," she says, shrugs and turns to walk away.

My mother is calling me from the second-floor window of our apartment building to come and have dinner. The whole family is waiting for me, she says. Helen must be having dinner now, too. I guess she'll come down here after dinner. Well, that's even better!

Then we can go for a walk, get a couple of ice cream sundaes, maybe go to a movie. Okay, Helen honey, see you after dinner.

Still, I look north on Old Bergen Road, in the direction from which she would have to come, just in case. There she is! I see her coming down the street a block away! I feel that tickling sensation in my stomach…

…No, damn it. It isn't her, after all.

Funny, it's October, but it's still mild. The leaves on some of the trees across the street in Columbia Park are still green, although now I notice some leaves turning yellow or red, here and there. I search the distance for about a minute, I don't want to take a chance on missing her. No, she's nowhere in sight; she must be having her dinner now.

I'll just go in, eat fast and be back out in 15 minutes. That way, I'll be here when she shows up.

One last look around before I go in. The sun is slowly sinking behind the far end of Columbia Park, filtering gold rays through the trees. Beautiful, but kind of sad. Why do I think it's sad? I don't know. A light mist has been creeping up from the Hudson River; now it's beginning to thicken. It's like a low-lying cloud, a white blanket over everything. I can't see more than a block away, and the trees in the park look like ghosts. I hear the sound of foghorns coming from the river.

I never noticed how sad the foghorns sounded, until now. Sounds as if they are moaning, like something dying. Funny how it almost sounds like they're calling Helen's name.

The street lights have just been turned on. The windows of Winfield Pharmacy and the Sweet Treat Candy Store are brightly lit. The bright lights usually make me feel cheerful, but not tonight.

One last look at the bottles of red and green liquids. Mr. Dorfman, the pharmacist, is counting out some yellow pills. People are eating ice cream sundaes and sandwiches, stuffing their fat faces. They look content, so content. And so smug. The girl in the red bathing suit is so pretty, so beautiful. She's smoking a cigarette and smiling right at me, smiling so warmly at me. She wants me to go in and buy a pack of cigarettes. Her brand, of course. I bet she's a real nice girl, in person. She seems so friendly, too. Maybe I should listen to her and go in and buy a pack… And, after supper, I'll be leaning up against the building, a cigarette dangling from my lip, like Humphrey Bogart, looking tough, and suave and full of *savoir faire*… And I'll look like I don't have a care in the world.

And Helen will come along to apologize.

THE SMELL OF LAND

Ed Perdue, in his heavy wool uniform and bulky but somehow drafty pea coat, shivered as he trudged toward the destroyer-escort *Rizzi*. He climbed the gangway, duffle bag slung over his shoulder, and saw the ice on the railings, ice on the steel decks, ice on the radar. The ship – cold gray steel – was encased in ice. His heart contracted with the sight of it.

Ed was glad to be going, to be getting away from there. Brooklyn in January 1957 was cold, too cold. The Navy Yard was its usual bleak self of concrete and steel, but this time it was all that locked in a freezer.

He consoled himself with the thought that in a few days he would be warm enough. He would be in the tropics under a blazing sun, among palm trees and sultry beauties. And there wouldn't be any complications, like the kind he suffered through with her -with Terri.

They had been married for more than two years, after dating for only six weeks. She told him she couldn't stand the long absences when he was away; she was lonely and wanted to be free to find someone "more stable." Ed suspected she had already found this more stable person while he was at sea.

The *Rizzi* cast off the following morning, moving away from the dock and into the channel, entering the East River and sailing close by the stately towers of lower Manhattan to starboard. The vessel slipped under the graceful steel-towered Manhattan Bridge, which gleamed icily as it passed over the mast, seemingly low enough to snap it off. Then the massive stone towers of the Brooklyn Bridge flew over the mast, like an airborne cathedral with its gothic arches threatening to collapse and crush the frail craft. They steamed past Governor's Island and into Upper New York Bay. The soaring skyscrapers of Manhattan to starboard and the crouching structures of Brooklyn off the port side were cold, solid monuments in a gigantic cemetery. The ship passed from the frozen womb of a dead world, through the narrow passage between Brooklyn and Staten Island, pushed through the Lower Bay and was thrust into the vast Atlantic waste where the grey waters heaved mightily and the icy winds wildly howled in his ears.

∞ ∞ ∞

The January sky was blue with occasional white cirrus clouds high above the vessel. The sun was strong. It would have felt hot if not for the stiff wind intensified by the movement of the ship through the sparkling azure sea. Ed Perdue leaned on the rail and allowed his lulled mind to drift with the gentle rocking and the slight rising and falling motion of a calm sea.

He thought about Terri, back in frigid New Jersey. He had been crazy in love with her. Still was, actually. He thought about her all the time, which made concentrating on anything else impossible. When he received a message by flashing light recently, he delivered it as "prepare to be destroyed" instead of "prepare to be deployed."

He couldn't allow himself to think about her, but it was hard not to. He had invested too much emotion in the relationship. From now on, he would try to forget her. He must forget her. He promised himself that, in the future, he would avoid sentimental entanglements. They were too complicated. They weren't worth the pain. He would harden himself, put on psychological armor. From here on out, he would go for sheer pleasure. No more complications.

∞ ∞ ∞

At first it was a mere thickening of the horizon line where the blue of the sky almost imperceptibly met the blue of the sea. It thickened even more and became a shade darker. Finally, Ed could distinguish, off the port bow, the pale lighthouse tower and then the grey-brown bulk of the 16th-century fortress to which it clung: Morro Castle. Then, from dead ahead to a point off the starboard bow, he began to distinguish the low, garishly-painted structures - green, yellow, white, purple, blue - strung along the coast behind the grey sea wall. The warm sun, the wind in his face, the sight of a land he had never known, excited him. His sense of anticipation caused a rush of adrenalin, a tickling in the pit of his stomach.

∞ ∞ ∞

It was a hot day in January. A yellow and purple blur of stucco houses, balconies and iron grillwork streaked past the taxi windows. The vehicle careened through the narrow streets, irresistibly sweeping Ed Perdue along with the current of Havana. His brain saturated in Cristal beer, he heard the radio blare the insistent, heavily accented rhythms and wild melodies of Cuba that compelled him to writhe in his seat and to beat on the dashboard in time with the pulsating music. The jerking strum of guitars, the hurried *chic-chic* of maracas, the rasping of the güiro, the shallow beat of bongos, the thunderous pounding of frenzied conga drums in different pitches... Strident, acid trumpets in a minor key, razor sharp, slashed through the alcoholic haze that helped him forget Terri and the frigid North.

Ed and several shipmates climbed out of the taxi at the corner of Pajarito and Peñalver, and confirmed that the name painted on the window was BAR VICTORIA before pushing their way through the green swinging doors. They stagger-swaggered past the bar into a large square room containing chairs and tables with black formica tops. Ed glanced around the room at the walls that were glossy black tile from the floor to the halfway point, and from there to the ceiling were plaster painted dark red. He looked at the gaudy juke box that stood against one wall. It was heavy, solid, brightly lighted. It looked like the focus of social activities, like the hearth around which families gathered in old Christmas cards - only different.

Currents of cigarette fumes wafted through what passed for air. Attractive young women in bright-hued gowns glided through the streams of smoke, like tropical fish in an aquarium. Detecting the white uniforms and leathery faces, they promptly approached the Navy men. Very pretty, Ed thought, but hungry, a school of piranha. Just what the doctor ordered: fun and games with no complications. Right: no complications.

Ed heard a commotion in the far corner. Turning, he saw a burly boatswain slap a slim young girl in the face. As she whirled away from him, the boatswain sent her sprawling to the floor with his foot. Ed, on impulse, rushed over to the boatswain and threw a wild punch. The boatswain blocked it and sent his fist crashing into Ed's face. Ed saw colored lights and found himself on the floor, tasting the blood from his own nostrils. His shipmates went to his defense, starting a general brawl. As he staggered to his feet someone yelled, "Shore Patrol!"

The slim young girl in green rushed over to Ed and tugged at his arm. She hastily led him to a back door and motioned for him to leave. "Gracias," she whispered, squeezing his hand, "you're okay."

∞ ∞ ∞

The next evening, Ed returned to the Bar Victoria, determined to control his liquor consumption and his temper. He was hoping to encounter the girl in green, the girl he had helped, but she was not present. He ended the evening by going upstairs with a voluptuous young woman who seemed to overflow her red gown and who had been pushing her pelvis insistently against his as they danced.

∞ ∞ ∞

The cool salt air rushing through the taxi window at two in the morning started to clear Ed's mind. He thought about the evening's transaction. The fact that it was just that - a *transaction* - began to eat into his consciousness like a corrosive acid. He had paid the woman called "Mamá" five pesos.

The Cuban peso, then being on a par with the dollar, it was no great sum. Yet he had handed over cash for her – in public - for the privilege of "making love." A very modest sum, but like at a meat market. No, not even that. It was not even like *buying* meat. It was like *renting* it. Can you rent meat? And after you chew and swallow it, do you give it back? Sure. You puke it up. When he and the perfumed barracuda in the red dress had returned to the main room, she smelled fresh blood and, without a backward glance, swayed over to her next prospect: a gangly apprentice seaman with carrot-colored hair.

Ed and his buddies emerged from the taxi and began to walk the length of the pier toward their destroyer escort, tied up at the far end. Ed felt the wharf was a tunnel between two rows of looming steel hulks, dark and menacing, overpowering in their size and proximity. A continuous hollow droning of the exhaust systems and machinery flowed from their metallic insides, as though the steel giants were moaning in their sleep, grinding their teeth, dreaming their mechanical dreams. Ed felt dwarfed and insignificant beside them.

At irregular intervals, puffs of steam hissed as they jetted from the steel vessels. Against the night sky, the small puffs of vapor were white – snowy white - pure white. Like human breath in a Northern winter, but much whiter. They would appear clearly for a brief moment, only to dissolve without a trace the next instant, as though they had never existed at all. How can something be there, and then, in a fraction of a second, not be there? Without leaving a vestige, a residue, some sign that it had existed.

Ed inhaled deeply. The cool salt breeze wrestled with the heat still radiating from the land and with the clinging odors of raw tobacco leaf, human sweat, cheap perfume and disinfectant. The fresh, clean smell of the open sea was locked in combat with the rotting tang of tropical earth and the stink of decaying vegetation.

When they reached their ship, Ed gazed out at the bay. It was black. The sky was black, but the bay was even blacker. It was a slick, oily blackness, a shiny blackness that glowed and reflected the moonlight like a black jewel. Ed saw the tiny specks of light around the edges of the bay where he knew ships must be docked, and at different points within the bay where vessels would be anchored. The lights were pale and sickly yellow when compared with the bright blue-white sparkle of the stars overhead, but the stars glinted hard as diamonds, cold as ice.

Ed felt strangely suspended in time and space. He felt as though he were one of the lights in the bay, swaying in the darkness under the illusion of motion, circling in place. No, he was one of the stars, isolated in the most remote and frigid regions of outer space.

∞ ∞ ∞

The following day, Ed and several buddies took the bus to La Concha beach. After a swim, Ed lay on the shore feeling the sand against his back, watching the yachts at anchor as they swayed gently on the water. He detected a pungent, sweet aroma carried by the breeze. A man had cut open a pineapple and was distributing pieces to his family. He heard what sounded like Elvis Presley's voice issuing from a radio. The tune was familiar, but the words were in Spanish. It was a local imitation of the American entertainer. He could have sworn it was Elvis. He could have sworn it was the real thing, but it wasn't. It was an imitation – a good imitation – but an imitation nonetheless.

Ed closed his eyes. He could hear the rhythmic shushing of the surf. A fragrant amalgam of land smells - tropical fruits, flowers, grilled meat, suntan lotion - alternated with draughts of salty ocean air. The sun's warmth was penetrating. Tempered by the cool sea breezes, it lulled him into drowsiness. He saw nothing but the pink of sunlight filtering through his closed eyelids. He was conscious of the soft terrycloth towel against his cheek, of its clean laundry smell. Terrycloth, Terry Cloth, Terri... In his state of revery, Terri's face materialized, only to metamorphose into that of the slim girl in green, the one the boatswain had mistreated at the Bar Victoria. She was not like the lady in red. The slim girl was delicate, fragile.

∞ ∞ ∞

Ed walked into the room and peered through the cigarette smoke. She was on the other side of the room, but immediately caught his eye. As she approached, he felt a rush of adrenalin, a tickling in the pit of his stomach. She was very young and slender, but with the basic feminine outline: narrow waist gently widening out to rounded hips. For an instant, he flashed back to his high school prom.

Dark brown hair, eyes like two drops of chocolate and skin the color of honey – her face, pretty as an angel's. Angels? Here? She walked straight toward him in her strapless green party dress, her red pumps clicking on the black vinyl floor tiles. When she reached him, she peered into his eyes and smoothly slipped her hand into his.

Ed said, "I guess you want me to buy you a drink."

"Only if you want to, sailor."

"Problem is, I don't have enough for both drinks and for you. It's one or the other."

"Make it the other, eh? Who wants to drink, anyway?" she said.

"That's all we ever do here…well, *almost* all we do." She looked sheepish. "There's no charge for dancing, you know. We can be very generous, no?"

They sat and talked, heedless of the rapid beat of guaracha, merengue, mambo, guaguancó – those dynamic dances that ordinarily would irresistibly draw Ed to the dance floor. By unspoken agreement, they danced only to boleros – those slow, romantic dances, never just instrumental, always with sentimental lyrics. They swayed lightly to the music, cheek-to-cheek, holding each other close in a rhythmic embrace.

At one point, Ed seated himself while the girl sat on the table looking down at him. Tenderly? He wondered. More likely with dollar signs in her eyes, he decided.

Her legs were crossed. He looked at her graceful little foot in the high-heeled red pump, her trim ankle, the curve of her calf as it widened upward, the rounded triangle of her knee, the rustling crinoline petticoats - that crisp, starched, white cloud topped by the lustrous green of her gown - whispered to him of hidden treasure. He wanted to go with her right then, but thought everything would be over that much sooner if he did. After all, there were plenty of other customers. And he didn't want it to end just yet.

To prolong his time with her, Ed told her the story of his life – somewhat distorted and embellished for effect – and she responded by telling him hers.

Her name was Vikki. After her father had died, less than two years earlier, her mother encouraged her to leave the countryside and relocate to Havana. In the big city, she would be able to look for a job, to live decently, instead of being a dirt-poor *guajira*, a peasant, like her mother.

She had gone to Havana and, not knowing how to do anything but cook and clean house, she had found a job as a maid in a rich man's home. Her employer insisted ("naturally," she commented) on her sleeping with him as part of her duties whenever his wife and three children were away. Finally, she decided that it would be better, if she had to give her body to a man she didn't love, to do it for decent pay…and where she wouldn't have to cook and clean house for a whole family, someone else's family.

It made sense to Ed.

Ed thought of the brawl he had started on her account. "Vikki, why did that bos'n slap you around the other night?"

She frowned, but said nothing.

"Come on, Vikki. What was it all about?"

She looked down at the table for several seconds, then spoke in flat tones. "He said I wasn't worth the money, that I was a 'cold fish.'" Suddenly, she looked at Ed and said, "Ed, I like you. A lot. You know?"

"Why?" A stupid question, he realized.

"Why? What do you mean, why? You're a nice guy. Besides, you may not exactly be a movie star," she smiled, "but you're not too bad looking, either."

Ed began to smile, but stopped himself immediately and laughed a short, dry laugh.

Vikki said, "Ed, I mean it!" and wrapped her arms around his neck, drawing his head to her diminutive breast. "Come on, Ed. Don't be like that."

In spite of his wish to prolong his time with her as much as possible, his will was weakening. He looked into her dark brown eyes, her sweet-serious face, her hands, her legs, her knees, the glossy green fabric, the crinolines...

He whispered, "Let's go, Vikki. Okay?"

She beamed. "¡Sí, Ed, muy bien!" She looked around and called out to an older woman, "¡Mamá, ven acá!"

The woman lumbered over, extended her hand to Ed, palm up. "Cinco pesos."

He told her he had no more than three. "Then forget it, sailor. It's not good enough." She turned to walk away.

"Wait, Mamá," Vikki cried, catching her arm. "Would it be all right if he pays *four* pesos?"

The older woman said nothing, but stared menacingly at Vikki's hand on her arm. When Vikki released her grip, Mamá curtly rasped, "But he doesn't have four."

"But would it be all right?" Vikki pleaded.

Vikki looked at the floor and mumbled something.

"What? I couldn't hear you."

Vikki sighed with exasperation. "I said I'll take care of the extra peso myself."

The woman looked puzzled for a moment. Then she shrugged and asked Vikki and Ed to wait a moment. Ed stared at Vikki. "What did you go and do that for?"

Vikki looked at the floor. "Because I felt like it, that's why."

Through the cigarette fumes, Ed spotted the woman in red. She was sitting at a table energetically kissing and embracing a young sailor who was stroking her breasts. The sailor's eyes were closed with rapture, but hers were wide open. She glanced at her watch, then checked it against the wall clock. With her current prospect still joined to her at the mouth, she noticed Ed and winked.

It was dark in the room, but their eyes gradually became accustomed to the gloom. They tenderly kissed and touched for a long while, her arms encircling his neck more tightly, drawing him ever closer. Everything was blotted from Ed's mind but Vikki.

Nothing existed but Vikki.

∞ ∞ ∞

The lights in the main hall were not very bright, but seemed so to them as they emerged from the darkened room. They had to squint because of the relative brightness, and their eyes smarted from the cigarette fumes as they entered the smoke-filled enclosure. Ed felt pleasantly weak and groggy. Then he frowned on noticing that the room had filled with prospective clients. There were large groups of U.S. Naval personnel, middle-aged American tourists, convention types in Hawaiian shirts and a few young locals. There were not enough hostesses to accomodate everyone. It was an opportunity for a girl to earn quite a few pesos, yet Vikki put her arm through Ed's and steered him to a corner table.

She looked dreamily into his eyes and murmured, "Ed, it was good with you. I love you, you know?"

"Come on, Vikki, don't exaggerate. You don't love me."

"I do, Ed, I do! What's the matter with you?"

"Look," he sighed, "it's just that... Well, you've been with so many men, so many times. Well, it's true, isn't it? That there's no way that I - or any guy - could have a real effect on you."

Her eyes hardened, became incandescent and blazed into his face for a split second. Then her features softened. She spoke defiantly, and yet with the manner of a patient teacher trying to communicate with a slow student.

"Ed, listen. You mustn't forget that no matter how many men we've been with, we are still human. We're women with human feelings, you know?" She brushed away a tear. "We do what we do to stay alive, but, once in a while, if we're with a boy we like, who is nice to us, who treats us like human beings. Well, you can see what I mean, Ed, can't you? *Can't* you...?"

A bolero was playing. They rose and lost themselves in the dance. They swayed as one to the guitars, the nasal tenor and the sentimental lyrics. Ed recognized some of the Spanish words - "amor imposible," "olvídame" - words having to do with impossible loves and with the necessity of forgetting.

Their faces were pressed together, but, from time to time, Vikki would lean back to gaze into Ed's face. To look into her eyes made Ed feel like a wax statue melting with proximity to a flame. He hated the thought of ever having to take his arms away from her sweet body, of having to lose sight of her angel face.

He forced himself to remember, though, that she was, after all, just a whore. It wasn't her fault, of course, but she *was* just a whore.

∞ ∞ ∞

Shortly after dawn, Ed stood on the flying bridge of the destroyer escort, heading out to sea. The early-morning chill was beginning to dissipate as the fierce tropical sun gained strength. The grey steel vessel gleamed brightly in the sunlight, too brightly. The ship was too clean, too neat, too shiny, too antiseptic – like an operating room.

They were making a course for New Orleans, but Ed was looking back, facing Havana. The brightly-colored structures behind the grey sea wall no longer seemed garish; they were cheery. But they were sliding away from him. He swept his gaze around the horizon and, except for the receding green of fertile Cuba, saw only a vast expanse of barren grey water.

The flat land on which the teeming city of Havana lay dropped below the horizon, but Ed kept looking back, gazing at the fortress of El Morro, still visible on its rocky precipice. The sea, broken by a bubbling, frothy highway of foam, leading from the vessel's stern to the fortress. That foamy path tugged at the pit of his stomach.

The land smell – a sweet fragrance of rain-soaked soil, of aromatic tobacco leaf, tropical fruits and flowers – gave way to the sterile salt smell of the barren sea.

WAX APPLES

    Yoko's pushing up against me as we dance, or as we stand here in the middle of the floor, swaying back and forth, in this smoke-filled, dark room, listening to phony American music. You can't even understand the words, with dead-pan Jap musicians in phony cowboy suits and a dead-pan singer in a red dress who don't even know what the hell she's singing about. Yoko looks up at me and asks, "You rike me, Sar-San?"
    I say, "Yeah, I sure do." She says, "So, you come with me, no?"
    I shoot right back, "Well, not right here on the dance floor, baby."
    She doesn't get it.
    I tell her the old joke about dancing being a "navel engagement without loss of semen," though you can't always be too sure. I added that last part myself. She doesn't get that one, either. And she keeps pushing up against me. I can't take much more of this. I feel like I'm about to lose some semen of my own any second now, so I tell her, yeah, I want to go with her, right away. She takes me to a back room where I pay this old lady she calls Mama-San.
    I tell her, "I got a yen for you, baby," but she doesn't get that one either. When the two of us are in the room, she starts to unbutton my shirt and fumble around with my pants.

∞ ∞ ∞

    Sal was home from Korea, back in New Jersey with Ed and Rhino, friends from high school. The three young men drove to Paddy's Clam House in Hoboken for a few drinks. Seafood was the specialty of the establishment, which occupied several large rooms. They went to the bar, located in one of the narrower rooms. They looked approvingly at the sawdust covering the white tile floor, seated themselves around a scarred oak table, ordered beer and became expansive in the comfortable old-fashioned surroundings.
    Rhino said, "Hey, Sal, tell us some more war stories about Korea."
    Sal flashed a smile. "Never mind about the war. Let me tell you about rest-and-recreation in Japan."

"Oh, yeah," Ed said. "I'll bet you've got some really good stories, Sal." Ed, eyes closed behind horn-rimmed glasses, leaning back in his chair, let a stream of cigarette smoke drift from his mouth toward the ceiling. There was irony in his tone.

Sal frowned and narrowed his eyes at Ed. He hesitated, then recaptured his enthusiasm. "Now you're talking! Ol' Sal made out like a bandit in the Land of the Rising Sun."

He automatically took a comb out of his hip pocket and passed it through his dark, wavy hair several times.

"I hear the prostitutes in Tokyo really know their business," Rhino said. The former high school football star passed his hand through the blond bristles of his crew cut and leaned forward eagerly.

Sal frowned. "Prostitutes? What prostitutes? I wouldn't know about them. I don't have to pay to get laid. Cryin-out-loud, they're lucky I didn't charge *them*."

Rhino's eyes widened. "No kidding? Hey, no offense, Sal. I just mean, like, it was a foreign country and all and you didn't know anybody and you didn't speak the language."

Ed raised an eyebrow and adjusted his glasses. "C'mon, Rhino. You don't have to apologize."

"Hey," Sal said, "let him apologize if he wants to. He knows better than to ask a guy like me if I screwed around with prostitutes."

"C'mon, Sal, give us a break." Ed sounded skeptical.

"What, you kidding? Listen. My first night in Tokyo, a buddy and me get ourselves over to a public bath house. They ought to call them *pubic* bath houses, if you get my drift. They're bisexual, you know."

"Who, the girls?"

Sal glared at Ed. Rhino looked puzzled.

"Just kidding, Sal," Ed added.

"You know what I mean: the bath houses are co-ed. Men and women use them at the same time."

Rhino's blue eyes widened. "No kidding?"

"Hey, would I lie? Anyway, like I was saying before I was so rudely interrupted, we get over to this public bath house and I spot this real cute little chick. Yoko's her name, it turns out, and I see her looking over at me all the time. Hey, I could *tell*! You know what I mean? I could see she had the hots for me, so I kind of sidle up to her, lean against her, skin to naked skin. Not face to face, I mean, that would've really been gross. I mean, it would show a lack of respect to the people there in the bath house, you know. I mean, we were sorta leaning against each other, side by side. I flash my Pepsodent smile at her and I say, '*ee-kaga-des-ka,*' baby, how ya doin'?"

Ed said, "You learn some Japanese out there?"

"What, are you kidding? Hell, yeah. I picked up a lot of Japanese out there. Firsthand experience, not out of a book like back in high school with Spanish. I picked it up on the street, in the bars…most of all, in bed, if you catch my drift."

"In the *futon*, right?" Ed said.

"In the *what*?!"

"Forget it."

Sal glared at Ed. "Well, anyway, this chick, Yoko's her name, she kind of looks down at her feet through the water, real shy-like and giggles with her hand over her mouth, like they do, and says, '*Genki des. Areegato gozai mas*,' meaning she's feeling fine, thanks."

"And she wasn't even embarrassed, standing there all naked?" Rhino asked.

Ed frowned and said, "Of course not, Rhino." He removed his glasses and began to polish them with a tissue. "It's the custom in Japan for men and women to take baths together."

"Hey," Sal said, "you know so much, wise guy, *you* tell the freaking story."

"Okay, okay, I'm sorry, Sal. Keep talking. What happened?"

"What happened?! You gotta ask? I'll tell you what happened."

∞ ∞ ∞

Tokyo. Good hotel. Public bath house. Big deal…no action. Some cute girls over there, stark naked, but everybody's real serious, no fooling around. I can't take it. I better not look at them, even think about them. People will see I'm getting excited. That would be too embarrassing, too damn embarrassing. Damn it, this is uncomfortable as hell! And the girls' aren't paying any attention to me. They look like they don't even notice I'm here. They're just kind of talking to each other about who knows what. I can't understand that lingo, but, damn, I better stop looking at them. I'm starting to…no, no, no. Down, boy, down. Gotta control it. I'm here in public! They'll see! Think about ice on the back of my neck. Think about that dead cat you saw, with the maggots squirming around in its guts. Think about algebra class back at Snyder High and old Miss Callahan's tremendous wart with hairs growing out of it. Damn! I better get the hell out of here. No one's paying any attention to me, anyway. A drag.

∞ ∞ ∞

Sal gazed off into space. Rhino stared expectantly at him, holding his breath. Ed finished polishing his glasses, replaced them on the bridge of his nose and leaned back in his chair. Ed said, "Well, Sal, what *did* happen?"

"Like I say, I'm really surprised you gotta ask. Anyway, you know ol' silver-tongue Sal knows how to handle women in any language, living or dead."

"You some kind of necrophiliac, Sal?"

"Am I a *what*?"

"You like dead women, too?" Ed smirked.

"No, you joker. You know what I mean: living or dead languages."

"What? You speak Latin?"

"Hey, wise-ass, you wanna hear this or don't you?"

Rhino was indignant. "Hey, c'mon, Ed. Let the man talk."

"I'm sorry, guys. You know me: I like to mess around. Go ahead, Sal. Tell us about it."

"Okay. Well, I got this cute Nipponese girl and her girlfriend to go out with me and this other guy I went ashore with. We took them for a steak dinner, one of those places where the chef stands right there in front of you and slices up the steaks into real little pieces, moving his hands around as he cuts the meat like he was shuffling cards or something."

"C'mon, get to the important stuff," Rhino said.

∞ ∞ ∞

Good steak dinner. Well, that's something, except I hate eating by myself. And that wise-ass gook chef standing right there in front of your nose like some kind of juggler in a show, slicing up the steaks into real little pieces, moving his hands around as he cuts the meat like he was shuffling cards or something. Just showing off. Annoying son-of-a-bitch. I mean, who gives a damn how he cuts the meat, just so long as it tastes good.

Walking down the Ginza, all the bright lights, all those neon signs with Japanese writing all over the place. Who can read that weirdo stuff. Looks like bird tracks, but in neon. It's making me dizzy. I feel lost, like I don't know what it's all about. Some of the signs are in English: Kozy Korner; Yankee House. Some are in Japanese, but with English letters: Ichi Ban; Sayonara. And all these Japs all over the place, they all look the same. I can't tell them apart. They look just like the Koreans. I feel like I stick out like a sore thumb. I wish I was back in Jersey City.

There's a red neon sign in the window that says GENKI-DESU BAR. I go in, what the hell... Dark in here, full of smoke. Who's this broad coming up to me? Not too bad looking – not great, but not bad. The band - guitar, steel guitar, banjo - playing American country-western. Good-looking broad up there singing. Can hardly understand a word coming out of her mouth. She looks bored, completely dead-pan. Doesn't look like she knows what the words mean, are supposed to mean. *Probably doesn't know any English at all, just singing the songs like they told her to. What the hell song is that? Sounds real familiar. Sounds like she's singing "Prease herp me, I farring, farring fo' you..." Another song, "Hai, goo' rookin', wa you gah cookin'..." This is too weird, Stateside shit-kicker music coming out of these Jap musicians in blue jeans, cowboy shirts and ten-gallon hats. They're just staring straight ahead into the smoke and darkness. They don't know what the hell it's all about. No expression on their faces. And the singer, too, a good looker in a sexy red dress, a short dress, showing nice legs, but she's dead-pan. She doesn't understand what the words mean. Neither do I, the way she's singing with that accent. Now, why the hell did I just think of my Aunt Philomena back in Hoboken? I was five years old and tried to take a bite outa that apple in the fruit bowl, but it was a* wax *apple. Why the hell did she have wax fruit in the damn bowl? And everybody thought it was funny, little Sal trying to eat the wax apple. Damn! Well, when we got home, my mom gave me a* real *apple. We always had real fruit in the house, no matter what. Ah, forget that stuff. I'm dancing with Yoko.*

∞ ∞ ∞

Rhino saw that Sal was gazing off into space once more. "C'mon, Sal." Rhino started to bite his nails. "Get to the important stuff, will ya?"

"Take it easy, Rhino. I'm getting there. Anyway, then we took them dancing. Man, mine was all over me right on the dance floor. I'm telling you, it was embarrassing. My buddy didn't make it with his chick, by the way. He told me later. Well, some got it and some don't. Anyway, Yoko took me to her place and introduced me to her folks."

"Her parents?" Rhino's jaw dropped.

"Yeah, right. Hey, you know, different places, different customs. They were real nice people – very polite, always bowing and smiling and everything."

"Were they scraping, too?" Ed said.

"Were they *what*...?"

"Scraping. You know, bowing and scraping."

"Goddam it, Ed, you're getting weirder all the time."

"Forget it. Keep talking."

Sal frowned and shook his head. "Well, anyway, like I say, they were real nice people. They gave me a couple shots of saké and smiled and bowed and she bowed to them. Then she took me to her room."

"To her *room*?!" Rhino asked.

"Well, what the hell did you think, we were going to do it right there in the freaking living room, in front of her folks and all?"

∞ ∞ ∞

They're playing a country waltz, but nobody's waltzing. Me and

Yoko, like everybody else, we're just slowly shuffling our feet back and forth, swaying to the music. Yoko's hanging on my neck, pressing against me, her long black hair covering my right arm. She keeps pushing against me, down there, to get me hot. Hell, she doesn't need to try so hard. I've been at sea too long. But that imitation American music is getting to me; it's phony.

∞ ∞ ∞

"Well, how was it?" Rhino asked.

Ed leaned back in his chair and said, "Rhino, give the guy a break. Can't you see he's re-living it? He's back in Japan."

Sal took a long drink of his Budweiser and put his glass back on the table. He looked at Ed and said, "No, no, Ed…that's okay." Then, looking at Rhino, "How was it, you ask? What, you kidding? It was terrific! She did everything. I mean *everything*. Know what I mean?"

Sal looked expectantly at their faces. Rhino's eyes were wide. Ed looked up at the ceiling and took a long drag on his cigarette. He exhaled the smoke slowly, watching it rise to the ceiling and dissipate.

"'Go on, Sal,' Rhino said."

"Go on? Ain't that enough? What else do you want? Want me to draw you freaking pictures?"

"I know what you mean, Sal, I think," Rhino said. "But I want to hear you tell it, is all. Just to be sure."

∞ ∞ ∞

Yoko's pushing up against me as we dance, or as we stand here in the middle of the floor, swaying back and forth, in this smoke-filled, dark room listening to phony American music you can't even understand the words of, with dead-pan Jap musicians in phony cowboy suits and a dead-pan singer in a red dress who don't even know what the hell she's singing about. Yoko looks up at me and asks, "You rike me, Sar-San?" I say, "Yeah, I sure do." She says, "So, you come with me, no?" I shoot right back, "Well, not right here on the dance floor, baby." She doesn't get it. I tell her the old joke that dancing is a "navel engagement without loss of semen," though you can't always be too sure. I added that last part myself. She doesn't get that one, either. And she keeps pushing up against me. I can't take much more of this. I feel like I'm about to lose some semen of my own any second now, so I tell her, yeah, I want to go with her, right away. She takes me to a back room where I pay this old lady she calls Mama-San. I tell her, "I got a yen for you, baby," but she doesn't get that one either. The two of us in the room, she starts to unbutton my shirt and fumble around with my pants, and here I am thinking about my Aunt Philomena and her lousy wax apples again. I don't know why. It just popped into my head for no reason at all. Those lousy wax apples.

CIRCLE DANCE

A bedraggled brown dog is blocking the car door as he chases his tail. He spins faster and faster, teeth bared and clicking furiously, almost reaching the tail. He growls with rage and spins even faster for a moment. Still chasing his tail, the dog finally moves away from the door, allowing me to emerge from the car. I tread across the brown leaves scattered along the sidewalk, hearing their brittle crunch, reach the shadowy portal of the stone edifice and enter.

∞ ∞ ∞

The man in the black suit with the Roman collar motions for us to approach. "Tomorrow is the wedding. Now, let's get this rehearsal right the first time. All right, the ushers and bridesmaids come forward. No, you don't hold hands. This isn't some dance hall…"

∞ ∞ ∞

Dance hall… Rhino and me, cruising on a Saturday night at Brenner's Hall. Girls. Plenty of good-looking girls. You never know how it will end. Can't wait to get inside. The excitement, the anticipation, an itch in my soul. Anything might happen, anything. At the very least, dancing itself – no thinking, just moving, sweating, burning off pent-up pressures. Letting off steam, steam generated at the office, at the desk. The desk is grey-blue metal covered by a green blotter. There's an antique black typewriter, an ugly, frowning piece of machinery. Piled on the desk are papers, piles and piles of endless papers, forms to fill out with the same meaningless questions, the same stupid questions, the same monotonous words repeated hour after hour, day after day, week after week.

Fill in the blanks: NAME OF CUSTOMER; CUSTOMER'S ADDRESS; CUSTOMER'S SHIPPING ADDRESS; NAME OF CUSTOMER'S AGENT; CUSTOMER'S AGENT'S ADDRESS; CUSTOMER'S AGENT'S SHIPPING ADDRESS; LICENSE NUMBER; TYPE OF UNIT; NUMBER OF UNITS; NET WEIGHT OF EACH UNIT; GROSS WEIGHT OF EACH UNIT; TOTAL NET WEIGHT; TOTAL GROSS WEIGHT; TYPE OF CONTAINER; PRICE OF EACH UNIT; TOTAL PRICE; SHIPPING CHARGES; SUBTOTAL; CUSTOMS FEES; SUB-SUBTOTAL; TAX; SUB-

SUB-SUBTOTAL; TOTAL; TOTAL-TOTAL; TOTAL-COMPLETE-FINAL-ABSOLUTE-SON-OF-A-BITCH-NO-BULLSHIT-REALLY-TOTALLY-TOTAL-TOTAL...

Hour after hour, day after day, year after year...another one. Another one on top of that. They dump one on top of the other as though they were unloading trash on me. The boss calls me Ed, *but I have to call him* Mr. Biaggi. *Fool around a little at the water cooler and he says, "Knock it off and get to work, Ed".*

Knock it off, dance it off, burn it off, laugh it off, talk it off, shake it off, maybe kiss it off, squeeze it off, push it off, shove it off. Yeah, shove it. Shove...

∞ ∞ ∞

"Now, don't shove." The priest is speaking. "Don't shove, ladies and gentlemen. All right. Now, the ushers and bridesmaids turn and face each other."

My partner has long dark hair and dark eyes. Nice legs. Sexy. She's looking at me. Maybe I'll get to know her better a little later. Damn! She looks something like Carla.

∞ ∞ ∞

Carla... A couple of straight vodkas washed down with Seven-Up at Brenner's Hall... Need some confidence before going into the dance hall, before entering the arena. Timidly swagger. Is that possible? Sure, timid on the inside, self-confident on the outside. Can't let them know you're unsure of yourself. So right: timidly swagger into the hall, sweeping a conquering eye over the harem. Rhino and me, a great team. I'd be lost without him. One throws the ball, the other catches. If one fumbles, the other one recovers. Brilliant wit, tales of adventure. Show them how smart we are, how brave. Dance, talk, drink a little more -can't let the fuel run out - dance again...maybe take a girl home...sometimes. But that time with Carla...

∞ ∞ ∞

"Closer together, closer. Walk up the aisle all together. Closer."

∞ ∞ ∞

"Closer, hold me closer, Ed." Carla's dark eyes widen and then suddenly shut. Her dark hair smells good, but blocks my vision. Can't see where we're going, but I don't care, as long as we're going, as long as she's with me. The most beautiful girl here...easily. How did I get the nerve? It's hard to do. Have to steel yourself, but, after all, it is my policy. If you're going to get shot down, it might as well be by the best. Then the defeat is honorable. If you die, let it be by the hand of the queen, not a peasant girl. By a noble knight, not some lowly pawn. By Don Quixote, not Sancho Panza. Be vaporized by a nuclear catastrophe, not struck by a beat-up Chevy. That's the idea. Something like that.

Besides, a girl that beautiful can really be lonely. So many guys are afraid to try; she might as well be ugly. But she isn't. She certainly is not.

She's smiling up at me. Her voice is warm. The music is soft and slow. The hall is completely dark except for the lights reflecting on the ball paved with little mirrors, twirling around overhead, bouncing the colors of the spectrum around the room as though it were a giant rhinestone. She's quietly singing into my ear. Her breath is warm and damp.

"Closer, hold me closer," she whispers. The floor is crowded and I don't watch where we're going. We collide with another couple.

Without even looking up, I mumble, "Sorry."

∞ ∞ ∞

"Sorry."

"It's okay, Ed. But, hey, Rhino's the one getting married. What are *you* so nervous about?"

"Who, me? You kidding?"

The church is dark and gloomy - even sinister. There are too many niches and shadows. The massive grey stones make me feel as if there is a weight bearing down on my chest. It's like a tomb in here - a mausoleum - and there's not enough air.

The electric candles mechanically flickering make the shadows dance off the walls. I look at them and feel like something's missing. Then I realize it's that comforting dry smell of burning wax and wick.

Electric candles. Well, why not? In the old days, they used real candles because there was no electricity. Still...electric *candles*?

I have to get out of here. We'll be leaving in just a few minutes, but I have to get out right now. I can't wait. It feels as though something's going to happen, something bad. I need air, right away. I have to get out of here...

∞ ∞ ∞

"Let's get out of here and get some fresh air, Ed." Carla is speaking. Is she really speaking? Are they really words I hear? Words or sounds, or incantations; whatever they are, they're weaving a web around me - a Black Widow spider web. The silk threads are smooth, yet strong and viscous. They envelope me, bind me, and hold me fast.

"Put your arms around me...now!" Her voice is an urgent whisper, yet it is commanding. She kisses me. Her mouth is warm, sweet, yielding.

Suddenly, she breaks away. "Let's go back inside. Now! Come on!"

Back inside, the hall is crowded, hot, noisy. She leads me by the hand to a specific destination.

"Where to, Carla?" She doesn't answer. She seems preoccupied.

Now she stops, as though waiting for something to happen. She looks across the dance floor. Why is that guy staring so intently at us – at Carla, mostly, but at me too. Now he's coming over, his face hardening with determination. He speaks.
   "Carla... Look, Carla, I'm sorry about..." *He stops in the midst of a sentence to look at me with annoyance. He turns to her once more.*
   "Can't we go somewhere private?"
   Carla stares at him unperturbedly, serenely, almost with arrogance, for a full ten seconds. Then she smiles. "Tony, you stubborn... It's about time!"
   She turns to me and cooly, off-handedly, says, "Thanks for the dance. See you around."
   See you around???!!! What the hell is this? Bitch! See you around...!

∞ ∞ ∞

   "See you around? Of course I'll see you around." The dark-haired bridesmaid at my side adds, "I'll see you tomorrow at the wedding, won't I?"

∞ ∞ ∞

   Out on the street...finally! The brisk wind shifts the patterns formed by the brittle brown leaves on the slate sidewalk. It turns my perspiration to ice, sending a shiver through me as I walk toward the car. Rhino and his bride will be going to the Poconos, in Pennsylvania, for their honeymoon. Dull! Really dull! Then he'll be a married man, settling into dull routine.
   Not for me, no thanks. No, sir. Thanks, but no thanks. I'll be jetting down to the Caribbean. Adventure, romance, wild times, variety! Why in hell does Rhino have to go and get married, spoil a good thing. What a drag! For crying out loud, nobody gets married anymore.
   Here's my car. I feel strange, as though something is missing. Maybe I left something back at the church. Let's see. I've got my keys and my wallet. No, nothing's missing. I've got it all. How come I still feel like I'm missing something?
   I want to get into the car and take off, but a bedraggled brown dog is blocking the car door as he chases his tail. He spins faster and faster, teeth bared and clicking furiously, almost reaching the tail. He growls with rage and spins even faster for a moment...

CHARISMA

Pat Hanlon was a first-shift waitress who spent every penny she earned on lessons in acting, dancing and voice. On clothing as well, because she understood the importance of packaging. What troubled her was the lust of the powerful for unwrapping the package, for exposing the contents, for handling the merchandise.

"Well, Mr. Cox..."

"*Peter*, my dear, *Peter*."

"Oh yes, Peter. Well, you see, I'm really thinking of leaving Hollywood, doing something else if this doesn't work out."

Pat Hanlon took a sip of her white wine, then brushed her long dark hair from her eyes. She struggled to affect an unconcerned air.

"But why, my dear?" Peter Cox, greying at the temples and moustache, peered intently into Pat's blue eyes and pensively savored his martini.

Pat looked around the crowded reception hall and saw the masks she had grown accustomed to in Hollywood. She glanced at the young men and women she knew were waiters and waitresses presently masquerading as poised contenders for stardom. She knew that while surreptitiously stuffing themselves with hors d'oeuvres and cold meat, they were calculating how best to enter into conversation with producers and directors. They wore confident smiles - after all, they were actors - as well as costly clothing purchased with money saved by scrimping on meals and by living in depressing hovels. Pat easily distinguished between these hopefuls and the familiar self-satisfied faces of the powerful: the well-fed, bejewelled moguls thinly disguised as kindly aunts and uncles.

Peter grasped Pat's shoulders and repeated his question. "Patricia, my dear, tell me, why are you thinking of giving up this exciting world, this glamour?"

"Look, Mr. Cox...Peter. You're a successful director. You've made a half-dozen films in England, really successful films, in the last few years."

"True..."

"Yes, and now Excelsior Films has brought you here to Hollywood to direct 'Night Errant.' Naturally, it's all glamour for you."

"Now look here, my pet, I've invited you to take those screen tests. And you have taken them, have you not?"

"Yes, but..."

"And, as I told you before, you have a good chance, a very good chance, of being chosen for the starring role." He paused briefly to study her face. Unable to gauge her reaction, he continued. "Do you have any idea what that would mean for you?"

"Of course I do. And if I get the part, I'll stay. And I'll put everything I have into it. But there are five other candidates. Three of them are already stars. There's Lana Swank and..."

"Yes, yes, yes, yes." He removed his dark glasses, extracted a yellow silk handkerchief from the breast pocket of his Saville Row suit and passed the handkerchief over the dark lenses. "You must try to be more positive, my dear. Yes, think positive. And remember, there are always elements to consider other than mere talent and luck, elements which, after all, can be controlled by the aspiring actor."

Pat watched him as he carefully replaced the dark glasses over his eyes. She wondered why he wore them indoors, in the evening, in artificial lighting.

He studied her face for a sign of comprehension, but found only puzzlement. "Look," he said, "why don't we go back to my place where I can lay it all out for you? We can't talk here."

∞ ∞ ∞

They had marched through the streets of Jersey City from Henry Snyder High until they reached the gates of Pershing Field. The students from Ferris High were already assembled. It was as though the jubilant but orderly multitudes gathering at the gates were a force laying siege to a medieval city. Ferris filed by, under the crimson and white banners, Snyder beneath the orange and black.

∞ ∞ ∞

Pat Hanlon gazed out the bay window at the surf washing over the shore below. They had stopped to pick up a porterhouse steak at the butcher's, and she had prepared it while he tossed a green salad. As they sipped cognac after dinner, Peter's arm around her shoulders, the director said, "You know, my dear, we are going to have to choose our little star for 'Night Errant' very soon."

Pat did not know how to respond to the statement. She could not seem overly confident. And she was certainly not overly confident in the face of her formidable competition. Yet she did want to demonstrate reasonable self-confidence. She hoped with all her being that she would be chosen. Not only did she desire fame and fortune, but she also wanted to prove to herself and others that she had talent and worth. Even in high school she had felt this need.

∞ ∞ ∞

The piercing fanfare of the brass against the brutal boom and rattle of the drums surged through the air. At the head of the Ferris band marched the drum majorette. A crimson and white shako crowned her long dark hair, which flew out behind her and across her radiant face flushed with excitement. Her blue eyes flashed and her smile registered triumph at having been chosen.

∞ ∞ ∞

Peter Cox said, "Did you hear me, Patricia, darling? I said we are going to have to choose our star for 'Night Errant' very soon."

"Of course...Peter." She hesitated. "When will you be making your decision?" She pronounced it calmly, with a polite smile, showing what she considered just the right amount of interest.

"Within three weeks, at the very latest. Much sooner, my dear, if things work out."

"If things work out...?"

"Yes, love." He spoke slowly, deliberately. "If things work out."

"You've already given the screen tests to all the candidates, haven't you?"

"Yes, my pet. Of course."

She ached to ask what more remained to be considered, what "*if things worked out*" meant, but restrained herself, thinking her brazenness might put him off. Instead, she stared at her cognac in demure silence. He watched her with great attention, as though he were expecting her to say something.

∞ ∞ ∞

In her white-gloved hand she brandished a long ball-topped staff, which she pumped up and down in time with the martial strains. Her white blouse was surmounted by a crimson bolero jacket. She strutted and pranced like an Arabian mare on display, her gleaming knees, responding to the drum beat, shooting to a level equal with her chin, her tasseled, white kid boots contrasting with the healthy pink of her rounded calves, her pleated crimson and white skirt lifted by her knees and fanned by the wind, revealing smooth, firm thighs.

∞ ∞ ∞

Realizing that she was not going to speak, Peter said, "You know, my pet, there are considerations you may not be aware of in choosing the star of a film. It's not only the way the lines are delivered."

She turned to look at him inquisitively.

He hesitated for the barest moment and then continued, "If the film is going to be a true success, a *hit*, one must be very, very careful in choosing the actors, especially the stars. Stars must have a certain *charisma*, something in their personality that conveys a warmth, an inner glow, a receptiveness to the audience, to the public, to people." He paused to peer into her face for some sign of recognition.

She said, "Go on. Please."

For the barest moment, he frowned. "Look here," he said, "there is a certain *magic* that can exist, or *not* exist, between the star and the public. That magic must come across from the screen into the audience. It is the same charisma that one can detect in the star's interviews with newspaper and magazine reporters, television personalities, even in the way they answer their fan mail or talk with fans. There must be a certain…how shall I say? A certain *charisma*, a certain…*openness*."

∞ ∞ ∞

The girls looked on in sullen silence. The boys, whistling, laughing, making wisecracks, craned their necks to see her. As she approached, however, they suddenly fell silent, absolutely silent.

Mr. Devlin asked Mr. Henderson if he had noticed the way the boys were gawking at Pat Hanlon. Mr. Henderson commented on the boys' uncharacteristic silence.

"You'd think they were in church," he said. The boys nearest the two men overheard the remark and marveled at the Snyder coaches knowing the name of the Ferris majorette. They wondered if she was having any effect on these older men who, they suspected, were beyond all that.

∞ ∞ ∞

Peter continued, "I have seen it happen a thousand times. We get an actress, or an actor, who does a wonderful job on the screen, *technically*, and who is physically very attractive.

However, she or he fails to reach out and grab the public by its lapels, make it *love* her or him. Why? It is because she - or he - is lacking in those innermost qualities of the personality that I have just been talking about. There is no *openness.* There is no *magic.* No *charisma.* And the public is aware of this. Don't fool yourself, my pet, the public is very much aware of this."

"But, Mr. Cox…"

"*Peter*, my darling, *Peter*."

"Right. But, how do you determine all that before putting the actor in a film?"

Peter laughed indulgently, drained his snifter of cognac, refilled it and poured more for Pat. "That is something that comes from experience," he said. "I haven't been in this business for so many years for nothing. Good heavens, no! But, you see, my dear, it is impossible to make these judgments without - how shall I put it - an intimate knowledge of the candidate, a *profoundly* intimate knowledge."

He paused to smile at her. "Then, tell me, my dear, are you willing to be open with me? Are you willing to put yourself in my hands with complete confidence and permit me to mold you as only I know how? Because, make no mistake, you must be willing. You must trust me without any reservations. You must allow me the most intimate contact with you, so that I may penetrate your very thoughts and feelings, so that I may gain access to the deepest recesses of your being."

"I'm sorry, Mr. Cox..."

"Peter." He sounded irritated.

"I'm sorry, Peter. I'm having some trouble following you. In practical terms, what, exactly, do you mean?"

"What do I mean!?" His voice became louder. "I don't believe it! I mean, for God's sake, woman, do I have to draw pictures for you? Listen. Read my lips. I want you to be mine, body and soul, before I can decide."

She opened her eyes wide and reddened with the pleasure of an unexpected compliment. She was speechless for a moment. Finally, she managed to say, "Peter, I'm flattered, really I am, but we've known each other for only five weeks. Marriage is an important step, a serious commitment. People make mistakes, no one knows better than I do. We'd have to..."

"Damn it!!" He bit his knuckles to stifle his rage. "Who the hell is bloody talking about marriage!? I'm talking about your ass, damn it, not your hand! Got that? Is that plain enough for you? You want a shot at the starring role, you get your beautiful little ass into my bed. Do you understand?"

Pat sat there, stunned, staring at the flames in the fieldstone fireplace, unable to move or speak.

"Listen," Peter said, "I'm sorry I lost my temper, but I'm not accustomed to people who are so *inexperienced* in the world of film." Then, softly, "But that's the way it is, my dear," Peter said as he caressed her shoulder. "You want to play tennis? Then you have to hit the ball back into my court." Peter rose to his feet and seized her wrist. "Come on, love. You're not going to tell me you're a virgin, now, are you?"

∞ ∞ ∞

It was too hard. She just couldn't grasp calculus. It was impossible. She would fail the course and not graduate from high school. She would disgrace her parents and end up a nobody. "Please, oh please, Mr. West, I've just got to pass. You can give me the lowest passing mark, but I'll just die if I don't pass. I'll do anything, absolutely anything if you'll only pass me. Please, please, please!"

He gazed at her, reading her thoughts, weighing the possibilities, the consequences. "Anything?" he murmured, stroking her long dark hair.

∞ ∞ ∞

Her senses had been pleasantly numbed by the cocktails before dinner, the wine with dinner and the cognac after dinner. Was this her last chance, her very last chance, after years of frustration, to show she really had acting talent? This could be the last opportunity she would be offered to justify her years of living in Los Angeles, of going to parties to speak with people who cared nothing for her feelings. She was weary of haunting the studios - the whole Hollywood scene. Besides, she had been accepting subsidies from her father since her divorce three years earlier. It was time to become independent, to be self-sufficient, to be a success. In a trance-like state she allowed him to lead her to the richly-furnished bedroom.

∞ ∞ ∞

The following morning, they drove back to Hollywood in silence. They both stared through the windshield at the road. He dropped her off at her place, saying only, "We're here."

She got out without a word. He made no attempt to phone her or communicate with her in any way. One week later, she found the courage to call him, but his secretary said he was unavailable at the moment. Even though she left her name, Peter still made no attempt to contact her.

The following week, she tried once more. He was still unavailable, but the secretary informed her that the starring role of "Night Errant" had been given to Lana Swank.

"You know," the gum-chewing secretary effusively offered, "Mr. Cox feels that Miss Swank has just tons of charisma."

∞ ∞ ∞

Pat Hanlon wrinkled her nose at the familiar smell of moldy furniture and felt the dank air clinging to her skin. She shuddered to remember how Peter Cox's beautiful head of hair with the greying temples had slid from his scalp while in bed. The suddenness of the revelation had not given her time to restrain a nervous titter. She glanced around her tiny furnished apartment in the Santa Monica Royale Arms and registered the broken venetian blind, the faded, peeling yellow and violet wallpaper, the black and white T.V. and the tiny kitchenette beyond, all hazy and distorted.

Her teary eyes lighted upon the scarred pine dresser with the framed photograph of herself in her drum majorette costume, standing between her parents, all smiles, and then shifted to her image reflected in the oval mirror. The lovingly-preserved majorette costume she wore still fit as well as it did in high school.

She placed the scratched 33 1/3 recording on the turntable, flipped the switch, carefully swung the arm over the warped disc and lowered it until the needle touched the bobbing surface.

The piercing fanfare of the brass against the brutal boom and rattle of the drums surged through the rancid air, reverberating against the walls. Pat's gaze returned to the oval mirror. A crimson and white shako crowned her long dark hair, which hung limply to frame her pale, tear-streaked face. In her white-gloved hand she brandished the long ball-topped staff, which she pumped up and down in time with the martial strains. Her white blouse was surmounted by a crimson bolero jacket. She forced herself to strut and prance in place like an Arabian mare on display, her gleaming knees, responding to the drum beat, shooting to a level equal with her chin, her tasseled, white kid boots contrasting with the healthy pink of her rounded calves, her pleated crimson and white skirt - lifted by her knees - revealing thighs that were still smooth and firm. Her blue eyes glistened with moisture and her sobs were muffled by the music, as she defiantly continued marching in place and pumping the staff...

The music ended, but she continued to strut and prance to the scratching of the needle on the record, faster and faster and faster, until she fell panting onto the worn, dull green rug.

∞ ∞ ∞

She had no idea of how long she had been sitting there, soaked in cold perspiration, listening to the scratching of the needle against the record, but became aware that it had grown dark. She rose, switched on the dresser lamp, removed the needle from the record, turned off the record player and lifted the record from the turntable. She looked at it for a moment and then smashed it against the pinewood dresser and swept the fragments off the dresser and onto the floor with one swipe of her hand. Then she stripped off her crimson jacket, her skirt, her blouse, her boots and socks, her damp underclothes.

She left the entire costume in a neat pile on the floor with the fragmented record and walked into the bathroom. After a long, caressing shower, she put on a pair of jeans and a sweatshirt, carried the record, the shako, the staff, and the pile of crimson and white clothing to the yard in back of the apartment house. She placed them on the grill in the barbecue pit, doused them liberally with lighter fluid, exhaled sharply and struck a match.

GETTING THE MESSAGE

"Gallegos must die!"

López struck the desk with his fist. "If that fool proceeds with his so-called reforms, the peasants will end up owning the entire country while our holdings are dissipated. And, mind you, Guerrero, it's not mere selfishness on our part. I'm sure you realize, my dear general, they wouldn't even know what to do with the land. The poor devils are like children. They need us to...to guide them."

General Guerrero raised an eyebrow. "Your concern touches me, López."

Noticing López's frown, the burly general dropped the sarcastic tone. "Come, now, López, you civilians always need high-sounding motives. That's fine, but save all that for the outside world. I'm a military man. What interests me is the method for putting it over successfully. I am still not entirely convinced that such a thing is possible."

López brushed a speck of dust from the lapel of his pin-striped suit. Then, attentively inspecting his buffed nails, he looked up and commented, "My dear General Guerrero, you're quite blunt. You understand tactics, but not tact."

"López, López, López...enough of this prattle." Guerrero sounded weary. He gazed at the palm trees swaying beyond the window. "You're not down at the International Journalists' Club, and you're not talking to your fellow civil servants at the Presidential Palace."

Guerrero noted the look of wounded pride on López's angular face and softened his tone. "All right, all right...you are not a mere 'civil servant.' You are the faithful private secretary, advisor, confidant and ghostwriter of our beloved President Gallegos. Seriously, I do recognize your talents. You know that. Otherwise, I would not even be discussing this matter with you."

General Guerrero paused to inspect the gold braid dangling from his khaki tunic, and then continued in soothing tones. "After all, you control all the communications media and, through them, you can influence both our own people and the opinions of other nations. I would not even consider this enterprise without your participation. But, remember, López, with all due respect, you need the Army to carry off any practical plans to dump Gallegos, and I am the one who has the Military in his pocket." He smiled ferociously. "I *am* the Military!"

General Guerrero saw that López gestured as though he intended to comment, but decided to ignore him. He continued speaking. "Now, López, I agree that each of us stands to lose a great deal, personally, should our great President Gallegos carry out his miserable reforms, but you'll have to convince me you have a workable plan before I can go along with you on this. I am not simply going to liquidate Gallegos and then take over with the Armed Forces.

"I don't want us to end up like Cuba. World opinion is important. And, no matter what you may think, the people of our own country are an even more important factor because - and you must never forget this - the Army is composed of men. These men have families, you know? Wives, children, brothers, sisters, cousins, in-laws, friends. And their friends have families too, and in-laws, and..."

"Yes, yes...you don't have to draw pictures for me."

"Oh, do I bore you, López? Well, just bear with me a little longer. I am a simple soldier, the son of a simple peasant. I like to have everything clear, absolutely clear.

"As I was saying, our soldiers have families and friends, a numerous and complex network of relations. And who are their friends and relatives and in-laws? Just who are they, eh? I'll tell you. They are the people, *our* people. And if the people revolt, are their sons and brothers going to fire on them? Well, are they? Tell me that!"

Seeing that López was staring at the ceiling as though to shut him out, Guerrero lowered his voice and continued in a more personal tone. "Maybe you think I don't understand these matters, eh? Well, don't be fooled. Now, come, López. Show me. Convince me. Persuade me. I have plenty of time to listen. Go on, take your time."

The thick-set man in the khaki uniform selected a cigar from the humidor on the impeccably-arranged desk of First Secretary López. He calmly passed it under his nose to savor the aroma, then settled back in the leather armchair. He deliberately bit off the cigar end, spat the bit of tobacco casually onto the thick carpet and leisurely proceeded to light the cigar, giving his entire attention to the operation. He impassively gazed at the cloud of pungent blue smoke drifting toward the spruce little man behind the huge desk, wiped the back of his hand across his bristling moustache and finally looked directly at López.

López controlled his irritation with the general's lack of diplomacy.

He realized that behind the provincial accent was a shrewd mind, and that the gaudily-medalled military tunic represented a formidable power. López, the attorney, son of a once wealthy land-owner, *needed* this peasant, this former laborer from the banana plantations of the coast, this devil who had reached his high position by means of his wits and ruthlessness. "Very well," López said, "it's quite simple."

"Even for me, eh?"

López disregarded the sarcasm and continued. "I have already taken the precaution of having a document forged..."

Guerrero interrupted once more with a sly laugh. "Forged? I am truly shocked, First Secretary."

López's eyes narrowed to slits, and the pencil he held in his hands snapped. "As I was saying, this document 'proves' that President Gallegos intends to utilize the land to be expropriated, not for redistribution among the peasants, but for the purpose of leasing to 'foreign interests' - the document does not name the United States directly, of course - allowing these interests to exploit the lands and the peasants on them in return for Gallegos' personal profit."

López paused and looked at General Guerrero for some sign of admiration or at least of approval. Seeing that Guerrero merely nodded, López asked, "Perhaps you're wondering if the forgery is convincing?"

The general dismissed the suggestion with a careless backhanded gesture. "You know your business, López, the legal material..." the general commented wearily. "Continue."

"Very well. You will deploy your forces at strategic points. You will arrest President Gallegos, the president will lamentably be shot to death...trying to escape, of course. And I shall take charge of the propaganda to appear on radio, newspapers and all other national media as well as seeing to it that the foreign embassies and journalists are provided with the proper report of the events. Gallegos will be thoroughly discredited, you will be a national hero and..."

"Am I not so already?" Guerrero interrupted, his eyes gleaming with mischief.

"...and I shall modestly and reluctantly accept your impassioned pleas for me to take over the government and guide our people in their time of need."

"Yes, modestly and reluctantly, but you *will* accept, will you not?" Guerrero smiled broadly.

"Can you handle the details of the military operation?"

The general said nothing. The smile disappeared from his face as he tossed his cigar butt in a high arc, which ended squarely in the wastepaper basket across the room.

López was quick to notice the purposeful silence. He hastened to continue, "Very well, General, let's set the date and smooth out some of the rough spots."

"Who else knows of this plan, López?"

"No one but Consuelo."

The general suddenly leaped to his feet, knocking his chair over. "¡Coño! Your wife? What the devil is wrong with you?!"

"Please, please, my friend, calm yourself. I know, I know, she is a woman, and women like to talk. Besides, they're too compassionate and she might feel sorry for dear old Gallegos. My dear general, you have such stereotyped ideas of women, sexist ideas. Consuelo is not like the females you have been accustomed to in the brothels of our lovely capital, or the ones you have...known...in the fields of your home province.

"Consuelo is beautiful and charming, indeed, but she is also clever, quite clever. She is self-controlled. She knows that what is good for me is good for her too. She knows how to 'grab the pot by the handle,' as you country people say. Actually, she will be an asset. She will charm the foreign dignitaries and the people will idolize her, absolutely idolize her."

General Guerrero set his chair back in place and seated himself. He closed his eyes for a moment, and then responded in a conciliatory tone. "Excuse my outburst, Mr. First Secretary. You are right, of course. I ought to know by now that you do not act on impulse. You are very methodical, very scientific. And of course you are correct in saying I am not accustomed to women such as she. I shall have to broaden my horizons. Yes, yes, yes. I can see that you are right. She *will* be an asset."

∞ ∞ ∞

The new commander-in-chief of the republic, President Miguel Ángel López, lounged in his leather swivel chair behind his enormous mahogany desk, rifling through the late President Gallegos' private documents. Methodically scrutinizing his predecessor's personal files, 27 hours after Gallegos' death and precisely ten hours after López's mildly exuberant acceptance speech, the new president encountered a large manila envelope in the L file, with his name – *López* - scrawled across it in Gallegos' handwriting.

A sudden foreboding prompted López to hesitate before reaching into the envelope. He extracted a smaller envelope bearing his full name and an address in Geneva, Switzerland. A moment later his unsteady hand broke the official seal and extracted the document.

He found the current month and year at the top with the space for the day left blank. His overwhelming curiosity won out over his almost equally powerful sense of dread; he forced himself to concentrate on the neatly typed message. Beads of perspiration appeared on his customarily cool brow as he read.

>Sr. don Miguel-Ángel López Marín
>
>First Secretary of the Republic
>
>My Dear Friend López:
>
>You will be in Switzerland as my Ambassador Plenipotentiary when you open these sealed orders. Although you will be comfortable in your new assignment, you will doubtless wonder at my reticence in disclosing the real purpose for your transferral to a point so distant from your beloved homeland (and I have no doubt you are aware of there being a motive other than the official one). My heart is heavy at having to inform you of the true situation, but I know you will understand and trust my judgment.
>
>To come directly to the point, our General Guerrero has made it clear, in his peasant frankness (and pardon my own bluntness), that he covets your loyal wife.
>
>You may be outraged at my choice of solution in this matter; however, I beg you to understand, dear friend, the delicacy of my position. While you are my most trusted friend and invaluable aide, Guerrero is unmatched in our nation for military capabilities. He enjoys the complete confidence of the Army (justly so) and is of the utmost importance to the security of the state in our present border difficulties with our "good neighbors" to the south.
>
>I know you are well aware of this fact; therefore, pardon me for belaboring it. I stress all this because I feel that your justifiable anger, upon being made cognizant of the general's designs on your charming wife, might possibly obscure your cool contemplation of the matter.
>
>Guerrero has actually proposed that I execute you on some trumped-up charge. In this way, he hoped to be free to pursue your totally innocent wife. Although he appeared to resign himself to accepting my refusal, I fear this excellent soldier can prove to be completely unpredictable in affairs of the heart. In fact, I sincerely believe that I alone, my good friend, am the only force on this earth protecting you from death at his hands!
>
>In view of my friendship for you and, at the same time my absolute

need of Guerrero in the present situation (and I emphasize the word *present*), I feel the only solution at this juncture is to put great distance between you and your honorable lady, on one hand, and our bullheaded general on the other. I implore you not to be offended at my disposition of this distasteful situation - a disposition which is only temporary, I assure you - and to place your full confidence in me. I am convinced you will do so upon reflection.

I feel it my solemn obligation to apprise you of this abhorrent state of affairs in the event something untoward should befall me; I cannot live forever, you know. In fact, my old friend, there are sound medical reasons which would tend to indicate a much shorter lifespan than I would have hoped to enjoy.

I cannot adequately express to you in words the anguish I experience in having to communicate to you this unpleasant matter. You will, of course, burn this document immediately after having read it.

In the certainty that you will strive for the welfare of our beloved republic while in Switzerland, as you always have done at home, I warmly embrace you and remain your most attentive colleague and devoted friend,

José María Gallegos y Sáenz
President of the Republic,
Commander-in-Chief of Armed Forces

The document trembled in López's clammy hand. His eyes involuntarily wandered back to the phrase: ONLY FORCE ON THIS EARTH...DEATH. He turned away from the black letters on the white paper, but saw the same words blazing electric blue before his feverish eyes. They flashed on the desk, on the carpet, on the wall, on the door.

The tramp of military boots echoing along the corridor riveted his attention to the door. Rifle butts pounding on that door reverberated through the spacious room. The presidential chamber vibrated with every blow, resounding like the crepe-decked drums at military executions. López's silk shirt was drenched with sweat. The words *ONLY FORCE...DEATH* glowed dully before the door, throbbing in time with the blows. Transfixed, he stared at the door. His mind could not erase that one word: *DEATH*.

From beyond the door, a provincial voice derisively roared. "Open, Private Secretary!"

INITIATION

It was in a vacant lot next to my grandmother's house on Summit Avenue, across from Pope's Triangle. The kid's clothes were grimy and splotched with mud, and his arms, legs and face were encrusted with dirt. He was sweaty and you could see trails of almost clean skin on his forehead and cheeks and neck where the sweat had run down.
"How old are you?" he asked.
"Five," I answered.
"I'm almost six." He sounded proud. "What's your name?"
"Eddie. What's yours?"
"Joey."
"How'ja get so dirty?"
"Huh? Oh, wrestling around with some kid. How come you're so clean?"
"Just had a bath."
"I hate baths."
"Me too, but my mom made me take one, said it would keep me cool on a hot day like this. She combed my hair, too."
He showed me a pink rubber ball. "Wanna play catch?"
"Okay."
We started to throw the ball back and forth when these two girls came along. I don't mean little girls, girls our own age. No, these two were what we used to call "big girls," which meant they were 14 or 15 years old. They were eating ice-pops or whatever you call them. I think they were popsicles, the kind that were double and had two wooden sticks as handles instead of one. You know, the kind you could split in two. They were orange popsicles. Funny how you remember these details...

It was hot, and the ice was starting to melt and trickle slowly down the sticks onto their hands and wrists, and drip onto the ground. The girls, all smiley and kind of loving, bent down to get closer to my face and began to talk to me. They asked all kinds of questions, laughed good-naturedly at my answers - even though I didn't think I was being funny - and patted my head. When they touched my head, it sent a soothing feeling all the way down my spine.

There was something about them... I had never before noticed the "big girls;" at least I don't remember ever having noticed them. But, this time, they made me feel really strange. They were so friendly, and they had such pretty faces. It gave me a good feeling to look at them. I couldn't get enough of looking at those faces. And their tanned arms against the light colors of their summer dresses - one was blue, the other yellow – and their curvy legs, the outline of their bodies - narrow in some places, full in others - even the texture of their skin. They seemed to glow.

One of the girls, the one with the chestnut hair, kept slipping her foot in and out of her sandal as she spoke to me. Her foot was so graceful, and the instep was tanned but the arch was a lighter color. Her toenails were painted red.

I understand it now, of course, but at the time I was only five years old and didn't have a clue. They were just ordinary, everyday girls from the neighborhood, but there was something magic about them, something unfathomable. They seemed to radiate a kind of glow, a force.

There was something in their speech, too, the way they spoke to me, the caressing tone of voice, the lilting intonation, even the quality of their voices – like silk or velvet. Listening to the music of their voices as they spoke to me made me drowsy. It was soothing, like when someone strokes your temples. I was enthralled, hypnotized. I couldn't move from the spot, from their magnetic presence.

I felt a sort of pleasurable irritation. I mean, I experienced pleasure, there's no denying it, gazing at them and hearing their voices and having them touch me. But all that produced a kind of irritation, as well, an itch in my soul that I couldn't scratch. It made me want something to happen – something – but I didn't have the remotest idea of what that something might be.

And as they spoke to me - it was mostly to me; they seemed to avoid contact with Joey - they would touch my head, my cheek, my arm, and smiled so warmly. Through all this, they continued to lick their orange popsicles, and suck on them, moving them back and forth between their pursed lips. At times, they would notice the sticky, melted ice dripping down their wrists and they would raise the popsicles to a point higher than their mouths, turning them so that the wooden handles were higher than the ends, in order to catch the drippings on their extended tongues. And they would apply those pink tongues to their wrists to lick the sticky-sweet orange liquid, so it wouldn't run down and drip onto their bright cotton dresses.

One of the girls noticed my gazing at her mouth as she held her popsicle to her lips, and, thinking it was the popsicle that held my attention, offered me some. I let her place the end of the tart-sweet ice against my lips and then I bit off a piece, the piece that she had just been licking and which had just been in her mouth. Then the other girl did the same for me. I was elated. It wasn't just that the popsicle tasted good and felt cool, it was something else, something I didn't understand, something ineffable. I felt a mysterious connection between myself and the girls, between them and myself, and something invisible, but immense and powerful.

Joey asked if he could have some, too, but the girls screwed up their faces and said "*No!*" in unison, in a nasty tone of voice. They said he was too dirty, that his mouth had germs. He stared down at the ground and clenched his fists. And, you know, it didn't even bother me. I guess I was too young to sympathize with him. I just felt happy and proud, immensely proud, that they liked *me*. That they had chosen *me*.

PERSUASION

By the end of her sophomore year at Paddle Creek High School, Diane Hunt had acquired the habit of chatting with Coach Mahoney before going home. The brown-eyed cheerleader came to regard him as friend, counselor, confidant and all-around idol. One day, in October of her junior year, she told him she had to speak with him on a confidential matter. Flattered by her trust in him, the brawny football coach pushed his thinning blond hair away from his face, settled back in his scarred swivel chair and waited for her to proceed.

"Remember that boy I told you I was going around with, Mr. Mahoney?"

"Sure, Diane, the kid from Tenafly. It's been a few months now, hasn't it?"

"Yeah. We've been going out since the end of July."

"Sounds serious."

"Kind of. I let him make love to me."

She quickly cast a sidelong glance at the coach's face. He involuntarily glanced at the well-rounded outlines of her jeans, and was surprised to feel a sudden pang in his guts. The coach looked into her expectant face, and with some embarrassment said, "Listen, Diane, why do you want to tell *me* about it?"

"Well, why not?"

He laughed self-consciously and said, partly to himself, "Yeah, why not?" He didn't sound convincing.

Diane continued her story.

"We did it on the back seat of his car on three different occasions."

Mr. Mahoney had a sudden vision of Diane sitting on the witness stand, wearing a modest dark dress with a wide, white, Orphan Annie collar, telling the judge, "...on three different occasions."

It occurred to him that it probably was not advisable for him to be listening to these personal details in the life of a 16-year-old girl who was, in addition, a student at the school in which he was employed; he might be placing himself in a compromising situation.

He also was puzzled because he felt a vague anger.

At the same time, these ingenuous confessions tripping off the tongue of this attractive young girl intrigued him, fascinated him, and he could not persuade himself to break off the conversation or change the subject.

"Did you hear what I said, Mr. Mahoney?"

"Oh... Sure. 'Three occasions...'" He tried to sound professional.

"I hope I'm not boring you, Mr. Mahoney, or embarrassing you. Really. It's just that what I'm going to say is important to me and..."

"No, no. Go ahead, Diane. I'm listening."

"Well, I really was in love with him. Or I thought I was. Anyway, he hasn't seen me or called me for three weeks, now."

"Gee, Diane, I'm sorry to hear that. Maybe he's sick or something."

"Sick? Are you kidding? Get real, Mr. Mahoney. Being sick doesn't stop you from making a phone call. Anyhow, some friends of mine saw him with some girl from Bergenfield."

Mahoney mumbled something about being sorry to hear that. He meant what he said - she seemed so vulnerable - but, at the same time, he was puzzled by the sense of relief he felt.

"And that's not all," she said. "There's more."

"Oh? Look, Diane, this may be too..."

"I think I may be pregnant."

The coach could see that she was searching his face for a reaction. He felt the hair on his neck stand on end. "Hey, Diane," he managed to say, "Come on, I'm not the one you should be talking to about this. You ought to be talking to Mrs. Berg."

"Oh, yeah? Why her?"

"Well, you know...she's a professional counselor. And, besides, she's a woman. Now, I wouldn't send you to Mr. Bagby, even though he's a trained counselor, too, but Mrs. Berg's both a counselor and a woman at the same time, you know what I mean? And she'll know how to help you. She'll know what to tell you. She has a master's degree in psychology. She knows about all the social services in the county and, most important, she's had experience with this kind of thing..."

"With *this kind of thing*? Hey, Mr. Mahoney, look. I don't *want* to talk to Mrs. Berg about it. I don't know her and she doesn't know me. Anyway, I'm not asking for advice. Not yet, anyway."

"But, Diane, I thought you *were* asking for advice."

"No. I just wanted to talk to a friend. *You're* my friend." She paused and looked directly at him. "You *are* my friend, aren't you?"

"Well, in a manner of speaking..."

"In a manner of speaking? What does *that* mean? I mean, I

thought we were friends all this time. Aren't we?"

"Well, sure we are..."

"Well, okay, then. This is the kind of thing you talk over with your friends, isn't it?"

"Uh..."

"Isn't it?"

"Well, yes, sure, but..."

"Okay. So, like I said, I may be pregnant."

Mahoney felt he was supposed to say something. After a moment, he asked, "What are you going to do, Diane?"

"Well, of course, the first step is to make sure. No use counting your chickens before they're hatched, right? I've got an appointment with the doctor on Saturday afternoon."

∞ ∞ ∞

The following Monday at three o'clock, Diane came to see Mr. Mahoney. Before she could speak, he said, "What did you find out? What did the doctor say?"

"I didn't go."

"You didn't go! Why not? Don't you want to know if you're pregnant or not?"

He was alarmed to notice that his tone was not as professional as he would have liked it to be. He realized that he sounded irritated.

Diane widened her brown eyes in surprise, then narrowed them to slits. She placed her hands defiantly on her hips, and very slowly, very deliberately, enunciated each word in a tone that seemed to indicate she was addressing someone of exceptionally low intelligence.

"*Mis*ter Ma*ho*ney, there *are* ways a girl can *tell*...with*out* having to go to a *doc*tor!"

She smiled widely, leaned over his desk and, her face six inches from his, looked into his face with amusement. He felt his face burn with embarrassment.

"Oh," he mumbled. "Right. Of course..."

∞ ∞ ∞

During the following fall semester, Diane Hunt visited the coach at the usual time, but the conversation was far from ordinary. After the opening comments on the weather and her progress in various school subjects, she said, "Mr. Mahoney, remember last year, when I was a junior and I was telling you about that boy I was going around with, and how I thought I might be...?"

"YES!" he said, just a trifle too loudly, almost shouting as he cut her off. In a more subdued tone, he added, "How could I forget?"

She gazed at him for a moment, weighing his answer, then said, "Well, remember I told you I let him...?"

"Hold it. Not here. Diane, could you step outside for a moment?"

∞ ∞ ∞

They were seated on the football field stands when they resumed the conversation. The pleasantly acrid aroma of burning leaves filled the air. "Okay, shoot," the coach said.

"Oh, I wouldn't ever shoot you, Mr. Mahoney." She was leaning against him, smiling broadly and speaking in honeyed tones, her face inches from his.

The coach looked around uncomfortably, and then said, "What's happening?"

"Remember I told you I let him make love to me because I loved him?"

"Yes…"

"Well, I realize now that it wasn't exactly like that." She looked at him expectantly.

"I don't understand. How do you mean?"

"I mean, I've gone out with another boy since then and let him make love to me, too, even though I didn't love him. I mean, I didn't feel about him the way I did with the other boy."

Before he could catch himself, Mahoney said, "Then, why?"

"But that's the point! That's exactly the point! Don't you get it?"

Once more, her smiling face was inches from his. Her full lips were parted to reveal perfectly white teeth. The coach felt an inexplicable anger course through his veins. He said, "Don't I get what?"

"Damn it, Mr. Mahoney…" She bit her lip and said, "Excuse me, Mr. Mahoney. I mean, don't you see that I'm not doing it because I love him, 'cause I don't. I don't love him, that is. I mean, I'm not doing it for love. I'm doing it just because, well, because I *like* to do it."

She widened her eyes and held her breath as she stared into his face, her lips almost touching his. He slid a few inches away from her on the wooden bench, rose to his feet, and thrust his fists into his trouser pockets as several of the members of his football team passed below and waved to him.

"Let's head back," he said.

"But, don't you understand what I'm telling you?" she insisted.

"Sure. You like to make love." There was an edge of annoyance in his voice. "Most people do," he added.

"Do *you*?"

"What?"

"I said, Do *you*?"

"Who? Me?"

They were almost at the doorway of the red brick building now, passing knots of students as well as his colleagues, and he still found it necessary to keep his hands in his pockets. He wished he had thought to bring his raincoat with him.

He said, "Hey, look, Diane, I'll talk to you tomorrow. Okay?"

∞ ∞ ∞

The following day, Diane brought the coach a piece of pastry. He bit into it and made sounds of approval.

"Hey, this is really great! What's in it?"

"It's pastry, you know. Watch out, it's sticky-gooey. It's loaded with honey."

"Delicious. It's so...sweet!"

Diane smiled mischievously, placed her hands on her hips and spoke in a slow, deliberate fashion. Her voice was seductive and edged with irony. "*Mis*ter *Mahoney*, there are things much *sweet*er than *ho*ney."

She maintained the provocative pose and the sly smile, and gazed at him as though waiting for some kind of response, even though she had not asked a question.

Mahoney was becoming alarmed. He was a 26-year-old man who was beginning to respond like Pavlov's dog to certain voice inflections and postures of this schoolgirl, although his response, rather than salivation, was tumescence. Being seated behind his desk, he relaxed and indulged himself rather than struggle against it.

"Diane, you're 17 now, aren't you?" He tried to lend a fatherly quality to his voice.

"I've *been* 17 for a long time now, Mr. Mahoney."

"Oh?"

"I'm going to be 18 on May 7th." She raised an eyebrow. "That's just a few months from now." She directed a conspiratorial glance at him.

"That's *six months* from now, Diane."

"Big deal! Anyway, why do you ask?"

"Oh, no reason. I was just curious."

"Just curious?"

"Yes, Diane, just curious."

She examined his face for several seconds and then said, "Uh, could you step outside for a moment, Mr. Mahoney?"

He hesitated. "Uh..."

"Well? Can't you?" She looked puzzled.

Beads of perspiration appeared on his forehead as he sat there, transfixed.

"Mr. Mahoney? Didn't you hear me?" she insisted.

"Huh...? Oh, right. Sure. Listen, would you get me my raincoat, please? It's right there in the corner. See it?"

She looked at him, baffled. "Raincoat? But it's not raining."

"Well, Diane, it never hurts to be too cautious, you know. I mean, it might rain. You never know."

She stared at him.

"Diane, the raincoat? Please?"

She shrugged her shoulders, walked to the corner of the room and picked up the beige garment. She brought it to him, expecting him to stand and take it from her hands. He opened a grade book and seemed to be deeply engrossed in it as he told her, without looking up, "I'll be right with you." He added, "Do me a favor and just toss it over my shoulders, will you?"

Her look of bewilderment instantly blossomed into one of recognition and then pride, but she said nothing as she followed instructions. She stifled the urge to giggle as he almost knocked his chair over, struggling to his feet while wrapping the coat around himself.

As they strolled around the playing field, he perspired profusely. "Okay, Diane, what was it you wanted to tell me?"

"Mr. Mahoney, would you say that you and I are friends?"

"Sure, Diane."

"I mean, we've known each other for ages now, haven't we?"

"Well, it's been about two and a half years, actually."

"Right. And we trust one another, don't we?"

"Yes..."

"And you're not married, are you?"

Mahoney stopped walking, startled at the sudden twist in the conversation. "You know I'm not married."

"Are you engaged or in some kind of meaningful relationship?"

"Diane, what is this all about?"

"Come on, Mr. Mahoney. You just said we're friends, and that we trust each other. Well, trust *me*, then. Tell me, do you have anyone special?"

"Well, no...not at the moment."

"Neither do I."

Seeing that he did not respond to her expectant manner, she resumed speaking.

"I hope you won't think me too forward or anything for saying this, Mr. Mahoney, but I've always liked you a lot, from the first time I came to talk with you so long ago. You do like me, don't you?"

"Yes." His voice seemed surprisingly weak to him.

"I couldn't hear you, Mr. Mahoney..."

"YES!" He realized he had spoken too loudly, had practically shouted. He cleared his throat, and in a more controlled register, said, "Yes. I said yes. Sure, I like you. You're a nice kid."

"Nice kid?" She looked down at her feet and said, "I'm not really a *kid*, you know." She looked up into his face and continued, "I'm a woman. I'm a young woman. I mean, I could've had a *baby* last year, remember?"

"I remember."

"So I'm not just a kid. I'm a woman. Anyhow, if you remember, I might have had a baby last year, and I told you I liked to, you know... *do* it...just for the heck of it. Well then, how could you say I'm *nice*?"

Mahoney tenderly looked down at this vulnerable young girl and searched for the right words. "Depends on your definition of *nice*, I suppose. I didn't say *innocent*, Diane. I said *nice*. I mean, you're easy to talk to, you have a warm personality, you're kind-hearted, intelligent, you never say anything nasty about other people, and, believe me, that's not a common trait. You're sensitive and, well, there are a hundred things I could say..."

"Say them, Mr. Mahoney. Go ahead, say them."

"...but the important thing, what I mean when I say *nice*, is that you don't try to hurt anyone. You're not spiteful or envious of other people, you have good intentions. That's the main thing. I mean, you're a very likeable person."

Diane wiped a tear from her eye with the back of her hand and dreamily said, "That's the way I feel about you, too, Mr. Mahoney. But, is that all? I mean, don't I look nice? I mean, I'm not ugly or *grotesque* or anything, am I? *Am* I?"

"Oh, come on, Diane. Gosh, Diane...no, of course not. You're not grotesque. Not even ugly. Not at all."

"Okay, I'm not ugly. Good. But, do I look nice?"

"Sure you do, Diane. You're very cute."

She smiled. "So, you could say you appreciate me as...as a woman, too?"

"Well..." He saw the earnestness with which she hung on his answer. "Yes, you could say that, but..."

"Oh, Mr. Mahoney. Then wouldn't you like to make love with me? I mean, if you think I'm such a nice person and all, and you think I'm cute, too. Then wouldn't you want to make love with me? *Don't* you want to?"

"Diane, for God's sake!"

"You're not answering my question. What is it? Are you afraid?"

"No! I mean *yes*, damn it! I don't know..."

"What are you afraid of?"

"Look, Diane, this is crazy."

"But *why*, Mr. Mahoney? Why is it crazy?"

"Why? Well, it's obvious. Look, I'm a teacher."

"Yes?"

"And you're a student."

"It's my age, isn't it? You're afraid because of my age."

Mahoney wiped his brow and said, "Well, yes."

"You don't have to be, you know. Afraid, that is."

"Oh? And why *don't* I have to be afraid?" He sounded angry. "What makes you say a thing like that? Don't you understand?"

"No one would ever find out, I swear it. No one but the two of us would ever know."

"That's not something that can be guaranteed."

"Mr. Mahoney, there are no guarantees in life, but that's no reason not to live it. You can count on me not to tell a soul, not even Jill Waters, and she's my best friend. My best friend next to you, I mean."

"Damn it, Diane..."

"Anyway, I think you really want to make love with me. That's the way it looks to me, anyhow. It's just that you're afraid of the law. That's the only thing stopping you. Don't let fear stand in our way, Mr. Mahoney. What we both want is too important, too *sacred*, to let some stupid law stand in our way, especially when I'm telling you that no one is going to find out."

"Diane..."

"Oh, *please*, Mr. Mahoney. You're a special friend to me, my only real friend. Just park your car tonight in the vacant lot on Merritt Avenue behind the stores on Center Street. You know where I mean?"

"Yes, I know where you mean, but..."

"Come on, Mr. Mahoney. You're not fooling anybody. Admit it, you're not wearing that silly raincoat because of the weather. I mean, look, it's not raining. And it's a warm day. And you're sweating. You want to come, I know you do. Don't be a coward."

She clapped her hand over her mouth, then said, "Oh, I'm sorry, I didn't mean that. But don't let other people, people we don't even know, tell us what to do. Not in something this important, this *sacred*. Be there at eight o'clock. *Please* come."

She looked at her watch. "I have to go now, Mr. Mahoney. My folks don't like me hanging around the school too late. They worry I might get into trouble. You know how parents are. So long, Mr. Mahoney, dear. See you later."

STORM WARNING

You know, there are storms, and then there are *storms*. And they don't all have to do with weather conditions. If only you could see them coming, you might avoid them...*if* you recognized the signs, that is.

Sonny Scoggins and I were on the fantail, just shooting the breeze. Suddenly, he poked me with his elbow and pointed to the horizon almost dead ahead. I looked in that direction and saw it. I wouldn't even have noticed it if he hadn't pointed it out. Not yet, anyway. The day was perfect. The sky was clear blue. The sun was shining and felt warm on my back. The ocean was a sparkling blue and almost as calm as a lake, but, when I squinted and concentrated on that spot on the horizon, I saw it. It wasn't much, a kind of dirty-yellowish smudge the size of your thumbnail.

"What the hell is *that*?" I asked him.

"A storm, a really bad one. Maybe a hurricane. I've seen them before and even been in a couple."

"Hard to believe. Here it is, a perfectly calm day, a beautiful day, and you're telling me that little yellow smudge on the horizon is a storm?"

"Better believe it."

I was on this training cruise to Savannah in 1956, around Easter. It was a patrol craft with a permanent list to starboard of about 45 degrees. I mean, it would lean over sharply even in perfectly calm waters, even when it was docked, for Pete's sake. So we really didn't need that storm, believe me.

I'd made friends with this other reservist on board, Sonny Scoggins. He was a great guy, a little older than I was, maybe about 28 or so. He was kind of overweight and African-American, or as we used to say in those days, he was a Negro. He was a social worker from south Philadelphia. I had to admire him. You know, those social workers sure as hell don't get paid much and they have to live in crummy neighborhoods, get into dangerous situations, sometimes, just so they can try and help people who need it.

I asked him, "Why do you do it?"

"Do what?"

"Social work. I mean, the pay isn't all that great and you can get into dangerous situations, drug dealers and..."

"Hey, man, I do it because I like to."

"Yeah, but why? What is it you like about it?"

He kind of thought for a minute, smiled and said, "They need me. Ain't nothing more satisfying than being needed."

A great guy. Now, to get back to the yellow smudge. It got wider and wider, covering more and more of the horizon and getting closer to us as we sailed on. About 45 minutes after Sonny pointed it out, it covered the whole horizon, dead ahead. The water was still calm, the sun was still shining, it was still a beautiful day. Then we went into it and everything changed. Everything.

The bow disappeared first, then the bridge, and then Sonny and I were right in it, all in a matter of seconds. He had told me we ought to go below decks, fast, but I wanted to see it, wanted to see what it looked like, wanted to feel it. In just one second, that beautiful day disappeared as though it had never been there. The sun was gone. We were in a murky darkness, strong gales, a heavy pelting rain. And we were heaving up and down, rolling from port to starboard. One minute, I felt my guts being drawn down, down, down. The blood pulled from my head to my stomach, while the next minute I felt I was floating lightly in the air, my feet rising above the deck. I was dizzy and couldn't think straight.

Sonny and me, we turned to head for the hatchway to get below decks, but the ship lurched and I slipped on the wet steel deck and started to go over the railing. The only thing that saved me from going overboard was Sonny Scoggins. He had seen it coming and had braced himself. He grabbed me by my belt as I tipped over the railing – got me just in time and held on. Saved my life.

Can you imagine? I had been just a hair away from dying. It's strange to think what a thin line there can be between living and dying – a very thin line. It makes you think. And it's strange how it can be a beautiful day - everything calm and sunny - and you might not notice the danger signals. In fact, you probably will *not* notice them because they seem so insignificant and so far away. But, it's out there, the storm, and you're heading straight for it.

When you're in the storm, it feels as though the whole world is in it too, even though you know that for hundreds of miles, maybe thousands of miles around, the sea is calm and blue and the sun is shining. That other world might just as well not exist as far as you're concerned at that moment. Everything's dark and dangerous.

Besides, you're nauseous and can't think straight.

Sonny and I made it safely below decks, but we felt real sick. I was thinking how you're just a little guy on that big hunk of steel that's the ship, like an ant on a metal bucket, but how even that big hunk of steel was being tossed around in the sea like a tin can, the huge grey waves heaving themselves up like mountains, the ship flying to the dizzying peak, then falling down into the valley, the wind howling. A huge wall of water comes crashing down on the deck, and you think the ship is going down and never coming up...that's when you feel the power of Nature, of God, and realize how small, how insignificant, a man really is. It knocks all the pride out of you. No matter who you are, how important you may be, you understand you're really nothing more than an insect.

Safely below decks, I wanted to puke up my guts, but kept straining to hold it down, even though you're not supposed to. I was weak and dizzy, flying up into the air like a feather, then dropping down like 500 pounds of lead...

I told Sonny how I used to like to watch all those movies about storms at sea, and used to picture myself on the ship in the movie, in that storm, and that, right then, I would have given anything to be safe and comfortable in a movie house in Jersey City, on Journal Square - or anywhere, for that matter - preferably, but not necessarily, with my arm around a girl, chewing on some Jujyfruits and watching the whole thing on the silver screen, instead of being *in* the damn movie, so to speak, feeling all the sickening sensations right in my own body.

Sonny laughed and shook his head. "Yeah, that's how it is with a lot of things."

"How do you mean?"

"Well, you know, you think you want something real bad, and when you get it, you know that's not what you really wanted. You wanted something else."

Two days later, we got to Savannah and I was all ready to go ashore on liberty with this good buddy, Sonny Scoggins, who, besides being a generally nice guy and was interesting to talk to, had, incidentally, saved my life. Let's not forget that little detail. *He had saved my life!* But Sonny started being kind of weird about going on liberty with me. I couldn't figure it out.

"How about going on liberty together?" I asked him. "We'll have a ball."

He kind of looked down at the deck and shook his head.

"What?" I said. "We get along pretty well, don't we?"

"Ain't that..."

"Well, okay, if you got other plans…"

He looked kind of, I don't know, embarrassed maybe, shook his head again. "That ain't it, man," he said.

"Well, then, what *is* the problem?"

He kind of sighed, raised his eyes from the deck to look me in the eye and said, "Look, Ed…" Then he looked down at the deck again and grumbled, "Shit, man, don't you know how things are in the South?"

I felt kind of ignorant. "Well, yes, I guess I do. I mean, I know all about segregation."

"*All* about it? Listen, Ed, ain't nothing personal…it's just that a white boy and a colored boy," that's how we used to talk back then, "a white boy and a colored boy just do not go on liberty together in Savannah, or anywhere else in the Deep South."

He saw I didn't really understand, so he said, kind of quiet like, "Just take my word for it." Then he looked up, smiled a strange kind of smile and said, "Maybe you'll even see for yourself."

I really didn't know what he was talking about, so I was disappointed. Here I had thought we were getting along fine, and here the guy wants to get rid of me, or so I thought. I mean, I was used to going lots of places with the fellas on the team back in New Jersey and some of those guys were black, or *Negroes*, as we used to say. And it was no big deal. Nobody thought twice about it. Well, no need to give examples to excuse my ignorance. I just didn't know what on earth he was talking about, so I asked him exactly what he meant and who the hell was going to stop us and all.

"Look," he said, "I know these places. I've been in these kinds of towns before. White folks go to the white parts of town and colored folks go to their own part of town. Ain't no use talking about it, I tell you. That's just the way it is, and I don't want any trouble. Understand? We can't go ashore together, so just forget about it."

∞ ∞ ∞

Just before the off-duty crew went on liberty in Savannah, one of the chief petty officers gave the whole crew a pre-liberty lecture. First he spoke about venereal disease and showed us these pictures that would make your hair stand on end. Actual photographs, I mean, of these poor bastards in the advanced stages of syphilis, with the roof of their mouths eaten away, with swollen dongs…and here I had just gotten over being seasick. The chief said the only sure way to avoid these horrible diseases was to "avoid contact." Then he kind of looked around the room at us and said, "Now, I don't know if all you geniuses are bright enough to understood what I mean by 'avoid contact.'"

I guess he must have seen some blank faces on some of those assholes, so he added, "That means *don't have sex*. Got that? Okay, so when you see some broad winking at you from some doorway, just think of these pictures and ask yourself if it's worth it. Or, if you're so damn horny you just gotta do it, for Heaven's sake, use protection. And I'm not talking about side arms." He thought for a moment. "Maybe you'd be better off going to a butcher shop and buying a hunk of raw liver to take out your horniness on."

Then he looked around at our faces, kind of laughed and said, "And if you come across some woman who's too much for you to handle, just send her to me."

We all laughed. It kind of broke the tension we'd been under, listening to the lecture and looking at the pictures. But the lecture and those pictures stayed with us, too.

Then the chief spoke to us about getting into fights with the locals, or rather, *not* getting into fights. The same kind of talk Chief Barker gave us the year before, the time my buddy Andreotti got us into that fix. Andreotti…he's still in that facility on Long Island.

Anyway, then the Chief changed the subject. "Now, a lot of you Northern boys aren't going to understand this," the chief said, "but, like I said, it's their town and we've got to play along with local customs. When you go ashore, you white boys stay downtown or in the white sections of town. Don't worry, you'll know which is which. When you see mostly white faces, that's the white section. When you see all black faces, that's the Negro section. Understand?"

The chief looked around at us to see if we could comprehend that complicated a concept. I looked over at Sonny Scoggins, and he looked back at me at the same time and nodded his head as if to say, *See what I mean?*

Then the chief continued, "And the colored section is a hell of a lot poorer and more broken down than the white section. You'll know, don't worry about it. And you colored boys, you're best off going straight over to the colored section of town. That way, you'll keep out of trouble. Down here, they believe that each race should keep to itself. And it's not just the whites. The Negroes down here see a white boy in their territory, they're gonna wonder what the hell he's up to there and he might get hurt. So let's just play by the rules, stay out of trouble and have a good time."

∞ ∞ ∞

Savannah looked pretty good, especially after having been at sea in a storm. Around the center of town there were these white wooden buildings - churches, banks with fluted pillars at the entrance - besides the usual two-story buildings with stores and bars at street level. There were pretty little parks scattered throughout the city, with grass, winding paths and benches, semi-tropical plants and flowers, fountains...and a lot of beautiful blue-eyed blonde girls.

But there was this smell, this unbelievable, heavy stench that hung over the whole city. It felt like it was sticking to my uniform and seeping into my pores. The locals didn't seem to notice it, but I found it hard to breathe. It smelled as if we were in a damn latrine, for Pete's sake, or as though there were thousands of month-old corpses stacked somewhere. Someone said it was the paper mills. I guess that was it, but the whole city, pretty as it looked, smelled rotten. Let's face it, it stank, plain and simple.

∞ ∞ ∞

I went out to Victory Boulevard with some of the guys. It was a beautiful road, lined with palmettoes and big mansions surrounded by acres of land with trees and fancy landscaping. We put in at this steakhouse someone had told us about. I thought about how, just the day before, I had been seasick, too sick even to look at a saltine cracker, and now, here I was, ready for a steak dinner.

I was putting away a big, thick, juicy steak with mushrooms, French fries and black-eyed peas, drinking beer and listening to Mitch Miller's arrangement of "The Yellow Rose of Texas" on the juke box. And the waitress would ask, "What y'all goin' have, honey?" in that nice, cheerful, helpful way. Back home in New Jersey, they'd have said something like, "Yeah, what's it gonna be?" in an annoyed, tired-of-it-all tone. Well, maybe I'm generalizing too much. Anyway, I was feeling great, really great, but, at one point, I wondered how Sonny Scoggins was making out.

∞ ∞ ∞

We were downtown, walking along the main drag, past a five-and-dime store. We needed directions to the U.S.O., where there was supposed to be dancing, free doughnuts and coffee and local girls who volunteered to be hostesses for guys in the Armed Forces. We stopped on the sidewalk and asked this man where the U.S.O. was, and he told us, pointing out the direction, looking a little nervous, now that I think of it. And then this traffic cop out in the middle of the street yells, '*Hey!*' at us. The man I had asked directions from - he was a black man about 50 years old - kind of widened his eyes and began to sweat. I mean, you could actually see the beads of perspiration start to appear on his forehead.

The cop told us all to come over there to him, right in the middle of the street where he was directing traffic. He said, "Just what the *hell* you boys think y'all doin' there?"

"We were just asking for directions," I said.

"Directions...?" he said, kind of suspiciously. "I'll bet. Where the hell to?"

"To the U.S.O.," I told him.

He narrowed his eyes and said, kind of slow and sarcastic, "The U.S.O.? *Sure* you were. Well…" Then he turned to the black man and said, as though he were talking to a dog, "Okay. You, boy...get a move on. Get outa here. Go on!"

The black man walked away without a word, in a hurry to get away from there, looking worried and kind of ashamed, I think. His face was all tensed up, like he was controlling a lot of fear...or anger.

Then the cop told us, "Y'all tryin' to tell me you were askin' that there colored boy for the U.S.O.?"

We nodded our heads. He said, "More likely, y'all were asking him for the way to some whorehouse in the colored section, now weren't you?"

Well, I don't know what business it was of his, but we told him again we were just looking for the U.S.O., and he sort of studied our faces and finally said, "Well, okay. But, what the hell y'all got to ask a colored boy for directions for, then? Next time, you don't talk to no Nigras if that's all you want. Ask a *po*-lice officer; that's what we're here for. Or ask any *regular* fella." By "*regular* fella," I guessed he meant a white man. Then he looked at us to see if the message was getting through and said, "Okay, y'all can go now."

∞ ∞ ∞

We finally got to the U.S.O. and really had a nice time. The girls were pretty and friendly, and had those sweet-sounding Southern accents, calling you *honey* when they talked to you and stretching the words out to a couple more syllables than they actually had. They were real nice to us, but they weren't allowed to make dates with us. They could only be with us right there, while they were on duty.

What struck me about the place was this: the second floor of the building was for the white guys and the ground floor for the black guys. Actually, it was below ground floor; they had to walk down a few steps. The black guys had to go to the basement, when you come right down to it. There was a big sign over the stairway leading down that said COLORED.

Funny part is, there were these Puerto Rican or Mexican fellas – some of them pretty dark – and there were some Asian guys – some of them Filipino – which is pretty dark, too, and these boys were up in the so-called "white" section. In fact, everyone who wasn't considered "Negro" was up in the white section. Hell, there were some so-called Negroes down in the "colored" section who were lighter than some of the guys up in the white section. Not that it mattered to me, you understand, but there were these little old ladies with white hair and faces that looked like they could chop through wood. These ladies were running things and had to make the decision on who was white or black. I felt like I was in another world. It was weird.

Well, anyway, I had a nice time at the U.S.O., dancing and kidding around with those sweet Georgia girls. There was one in particular I really liked. Joan was her name, and it seemed she liked me too, but she wasn't allowed to make a date with anyone. So, after a few hours, I took off. As I walked out into the street, who do I see coming toward me, but Sonny Scoggins!

"Hey, buddy," I yelled out, "I thought we couldn't go to the same places."

Flicking my eyes just past Sonny's shoulder, I noticed a few local guys down the block. I figured they were local because they weren't in uniform. They were walking up the street toward us.

Sonny smiled kind of embarrassed-like. "Yeah, well, I didn't know about the U.S.O. until a little while ago. They told me about it over in the colored part of town. They told me there's a section for us colored boys in here. Still wouldn't have been with you anyway. You'd have been up in the white section."

Just then, Joan came out of the building. She looked at me and smiled. She was about to say something when she looked at Sonny, and then tripped and fell. Sonny - I guess without thinking - bent down and grabbed her arm to help her up at the same time I did. The local boys were just a few yards from us. Joan got to her feet, mumbled "thank you" and walked away fast, looking worried.

Sonny shook his head. "Damn!" he said.

"What?"

"I gotta be more careful."

"What do you mean?"

The local boys - there were six of them - came up to us and one of them, a big guy in jeans and a t-shirt, said to Sonny, "You goddam nigger! Don't you know enough to keep your dirty black hands off a white woman?"

Sonny didn't say a word. He just looked at the big guy, not challenging him, but not looking down at the ground either. He just looked him in the eye with no expression at all on his face, like he was thinking it was no use talking. He was going to wait and see what would happen. I'm sure he must have been worried, but had too much self-respect to show it. I know *I* was *damn* worried.

I said to the big guy, "For Pete's sake, the man was just helping her get up after she fell down."

Sonny gave me a kind of warning look.

The locals crowded in closer. "Who the hell was asking *you* anything, you fuckin' nigger-lovin' Yankee shit of a sailor boy! Y'all think you can come down here with your fancy uniforms and your money and do whatever the hell you want?"

I said, "Look, guys, we were minding our own business when the girl fell down and this man and I just..."

"This man?" the big guy said. "Yeah, I know what y'all were doin'. You and this nigger boy here put your hands all over her. Felt her up real good is what you did. Well, she's one of *our* women, not yours, and sure as hell not *yours*, nigger." He looked back at Sonny.

Sonny didn't say a word; he just stared straight ahead. The big guy wasn't getting any satisfaction, I guess, so he took a swing at Sonny. Sonny ducked and put up his hands as if to say he wasn't looking for a fight. One of the others got behind Sonny and grabbed his arms. The big guy punched Sonny in the midsection. I took a swing at the big guy and landed one on his jaw, but the six of them were all over us. I think they might've killed us, but a few more Navy men came along and joined in on our side. Well, before the Shore Patrol got there to break it up, Sonny and I were a mess. I had a bloody nose and a chipped tooth, and Sonny had swollen eyes, a split lip and a broken arm.

∞ ∞ ∞

The next morning, I was up on the bridge, polishing the brass, thinking about what had happened. My whole body ached pretty bad. There we were, our old scow docked on the Savannah River, tied up alongside the old concrete quay along with all these other ships, like cars parked along a curb. There was this clean, white Coast Guard craft docked astern of us; it was the *Aurora*, I remember. I was looking at the weathered, grey stone buildings along the pier. South Carolina was way across the other side of the Savannah River. You could hardly see it because of the distance, the sun's glare on the water and the steamy haze. I looked back at the decaying buildings on the pier and caught that rotten smell in the air. That stink gave me a bad feeling, a really bad feeling.

And, you know, every time I think about what happened in Savannah, I can't help thinking about that storm, when Sonny Scoggins saved my life. I don't know why I can't think of one thing without the other popping into my head, as if there were some kind of connection, even though I know there isn't any. I mean, the fight was one thing and the storm something else altogether – besides the fact that Sonny was involved in both of them, that is.

I think about the fight in front of the U.S.O. in Savannah, or even that traffic cop, and then - zoom - I'm back on the patrol craft, the sun is shining and feels good, the sky is clear blue, and the ocean is even bluer and sparkling and just as calm as a lake...and then I see that dirty-yellowish smudge no bigger than my thumbnail way off on the horizon and I get this really bad feeling in my gut, like something is going to happen, something terrible.

    The yellow smudge doesn't seem like anything at all, and you wouldn't even notice it if someone didn't point it out to you. But it's there, all right, and you're heading straight for it...

SHAME

I couldn't have been more than six or seven years old. We were living in the Bronx then. I was leaning against a telephone pole on Andrews Avenue near 175th Street with my hands in my pockets. None of my friends were around. I didn't even live in this neighborhood; my mother took me there so she could visit her cousin. Well, Mom was talking to her cousin and some other woman, and I was feeling out of place, with nothing to do, no one I knew around…and there was this girl. She must have been about nine or maybe even ten years old, sitting on a wooden folding chair near the curb, crocheting, or whatever-the-heck you call it. She had this little wooden cylinder with tiny metal loops around the top and she was feeding yarn into the top and a kind of braid was coming out the bottom.

This girl had long dark hair – reached right down past her shoulders, halfway down her back. It was beautiful, her hair, real smooth and shiny. Now that I think about it, she must have spent a lot of time combing and brushing it, or somebody did it for her. She had a face that I guess I would now call *interesting* or even *intriguing*; anyway, it sure intrigued me at the time. I felt it was a "grown-up" face, a woman's face, rather than a little girl's face. It's hard to explain.

While she was working with her yarn, she would look up at me every once in a while. When I think about it now, I guess it was because I was staring at her. Now, the only reason I was staring at her was because she had that quality in her face, her eyes, that fascinated me. I must have been about three yards away from her.

Anyway, there was something about that girl that, today, I would call *exciting*. Now, her face wasn't what you'd call *pretty*, like Shirley Temple's or like a doll's; it was attractive in a more serious way, a deeper way, y'know? After she looked up from her work a few times to find me staring at her, this one time she looked me squarely in the eye for a full five or six seconds, I'd say. It gave me a real sensation, a thrill, to see that she noticed me. And she said, frank and straightforward as could be, with a way of talking that seemed…well…*sophisticated*, I guess, she said, "Do you like girls?"

She didn't smile or look particularly friendly when she asked that question; she seemed non-committal, I guess, and serious, very serious. Well, that question really took me by surprise. I must have mulled it over in my mind for a full minute - that's a whole 60 seconds, which can be a whole lot longer than you might imagine - before I answered her.

You see, the question represented a serious problem. If by *girls* she meant girls my own age - or even most girls *her* age - the answer, in all honesty, was *no*. But, if what she meant was the "big girls," as we called the teenagers, then the answer was a definite *yes*, though I didn't want to go around telling the whole world about it. Somehow, I felt it would've been something to be ashamed of back then; it seemed like something to keep secret, like I was the only boy in the world who liked to look at the "big girls," and like you weren't supposed to. Naturally, I found out years later that it was normal; at least Ed and Sal felt like I did about it.

Now, as I said, I didn't particularly care for little girls, the ones who were my own age; you know, they were always pestering us to play with them, only they didn't know how to play the games we liked. Or they weren't good at those games. Or they wanted us to play "house" with them. Besides, they weren't much to look at - not like the older girls, who were actually gorgeous.

I figured she must have been referring to the little girls, since she was one herself, even if she was an unusual specimen of a little girl, as I said. So I didn't want to come right out and say *no*, because she might've been insulted, belonging to the same sex and all, you understand. And I didn't want to insult her especially because, as I said, there was something about her that I really liked, to put it mildly. So, because she was a very special girl, and because I was a polite little fellow anyway, *and* because she would be the last person I would've wanted to offend or have not like me, I had just about made up my mind to lie - something that really went against my grain - and answer in the affirmative.

I was struggling with my conscience. Or my conscience was struggling with my desire to please. Then another factor came up: I remembered that not only didn't I particularly care for most little girls, but that boys weren't *supposed* to like them. The other guys would make fun of you and say they knew who your girlfriend was, and your mom and dad would kind of look at you with that big smile…you know. I would have been embarrassed if anyone heard me say that, *yes*, I liked girls. I mean, it was uncomfortable enough knowing that this girl had caught me watching her. So, besides the fact that I would have been telling a lie if I were to say *yes*, I would also be letting myself in for a lot of embarrassment, even shame.

It was a dilemma. And, as I said, it took me a full minute to decide on a response. All that time, she had those clever brown eyes fixed unwaveringly on me, waiting for the answer to this monumentally important question. It was a great struggle, but I made the decision to be diplomatic - and brave, very brave - and to lie, when you come right down to it, by answering in the affirmative.

All this just to not hurt the feelings of this attractive little girl. And I say *little* in retrospect; for me, at that time, she was very mature, older than I was, almost a woman, almost a teenager.

I gathered up all my courage, "girded up my loins," as it says in the Bible. I'm not kidding; I mean, I really had to summon all my courage, believe me. After looking around to see that no one else would hear my answer, I gallantly pronounced the word: *yes*.

Well, hell, I expected, as you might imagine, at the very least to be rewarded with a smile for gallantry in action, from the object of my adoration. Right? Right. Instead, the little bitch tossed her head and said, in the nastiest tone of voice, "Then you're a sissy!" Then she went back to her braiding; it was as if, as far as she was concerned, I no longer existed.

I felt like crawling into a hole somewhere and disappearing. Yeah, me, Rhino Mahoney. Well, it would be a long time after that, a *real* long time, before I would show any girl that I liked her.

A TIME TO REAP

Carpe diem. ("Seize the day.")

    He crouched there, concealed by the brush, clutching his rifle. Squinting along the barrel, he watched the buck pick its way toward him. The bitter wind whipped through the bare trees with a whispering howl, searing his ungloved hand, biting his nose and cheeks. This was Ed Perdue's first opportunity to bag a deer.

    A twig snapped under Ed's elbow.

    At the end of the long, black barrel was the unsuspecting creature. It seemed close enough, but was partially concealed by a clump of birch. Ed would wait until it showed itself more clearly before he squeezed his stiffening finger. *Just until it comes into the clearing*, he told himself.

    The animal stood completely motionless. It was balanced on three legs, the left foreleg extended before it, slightly bent at the knee, the hoof two inches off the ground. Its head was raised, the black velvety snout quivering as it sniffed the air. An ear turned toward Ed. The brown eyes were wide in apprehension. The deer's soft body awaited the hard bit of metal to plunge into it and slam it to the ground.

    "Why couldn't it be a *tiger*, damn it!" Ed muttered.

    The buck sprang out of the thicket into full view. Ed knew it would remain only for an instant before bounding behind another clump of trees.

    "Now!" he told himself.

    The gun sights were lined up against the deer's breast. Ed's finger tightened on the trigger. A tremor ran through the animal's body. Ed's forefinger did not budge. The deer darted for cover.

    Ed laid his weapon down with relief. He rested his forehead on his arm and exhaled sharply. The crack of a rifle shot jolted his head back up. The deer crashed to the frozen ground, twitching.

∞ ∞ ∞

    It was a spacious hall, but comfortably cluttered. Oaken

crossbeams supported the low, white ceiling. The logs blazing in the massive fieldstone fireplace lent a cheery, though unsteady, glow and produced a mildly acrid aroma. Directly over the fireplace, a moose head stared balefully. Beyond the high, narrow windows stretched the grey skies and bare trees of the Adirondacks.

"So Ed, here, was aiming at this buck, see? It was just *begging* for it." Dan Turner passed a comb through his dark, wavy hair. "It couldn't have been easier if it had gone over to him and said, 'Here I am, Mr. Perdue, let me have it,' but I saw that Ed didn't fire…and it didn't look like he ever would."

Dan drew deeply on his cigar, and blew a cloud of blue smoke toward the circular iron chandeliers that dribbled a weak light over the leather and oak furniture.

He continued, "Then this beauty starts to run for cover and I figure, what the hell, and I let him have it. Got him clean, too. That deer was asking for it, and if Ed wasn't going to do it, I sure as hell wasn't going to let it get away."

Jean, seated on the red leather chair opposite Ed, stopped sipping her sloe-gin fizz to ask, "Why *didn't* you fire, Ed?" He was peering over the top of his scotch-and-soda at her face, softly pretty with its ash-blonde hair and blue eyes.

"Maybe he can't stand the sight of blood." Florence's pale lips curled in an ironic smile. Her dark, heavily made-up eyes narrowed as her filtered cigarette smoke swirled about her face.

"I don't know," Ed answered. "It's just that it looked so graceful and, well, defenseless…you know."

Florence spoke with heavy irony. "Now, isn't that sweet." She automatically smoothed her black hair.

"Just like you, kid," Ernie Waller muttered, his pipe clenched between his teeth. The logs crackled in the fireplace, the exploding sap taking the force of a comment.

Jean had kept her eyes fixed on Ed, even while Florence and Ernie were speaking. She said, "I know what you mean, Ed. Deer are such harmless creatures. And they have such sweet faces."

"Sweet faces," Dan repeated. "But not as sweet as yours, baby. But, hey, deer were made to be shot, just like girls were made to…"

"To kiss?" Florence helped.

"Ah…yeah, that's it." He winked confidentially. Then he glanced at his watch and said, "Well, all this is very interesting, but I've got an appointment with another kind of 'dear.' See you later, kids."

Florence stood, taking Ernie's hand. "Let's go see that fabulous bar they have here, Ernie. Okay?"

"Lead the way, doll. I could use some more of that good stuff."

As they left, Jean crossed over to sit beside Ed on the couch, turning to him with her arm resting on its back. Her light blue blouse contrasted with her blond hair, accentuating the blue of her eyes. She smiled with pink-orange lips and warmly said, "So you're not the Great White Hunter, hmm?"

Ed self-consciously cleared his throat and took a gulp of his highball.

"Are you sorry you came up here?" she asked.

Ed looked into her face for a long moment. "No," he answered. "I'm not sorry I came."

She smiled and looked down at her drink. Her face glowed a deeper shade of pink. She looked up and said, "Good. After all, you don't actually have to hunt when you're up here. Just getting away from everything is enough."

"You don't get away from *everything* up here."

"You know what I mean, away from the rushing around in New York, away from going frantic in the city, being somewhere where things are…are…"

"Natural?"

"Well, yes, that's it. Don't you feel that way?"

"Sure."

"Then, you see? You don't have to be a hunter. Florence and I didn't come up here to hunt."

Ed smiled wryly. "She seems a bit predatory to me."

"Well, everyone is hunting for something or other, Ed." She took a long drink of the red liquid.

Ed's gaze ran down her arm to the delicate hand resting on the back of the couch. Her fingernails were shiny clean. White tips on pink nails. Her skin looked smooth. He tried to imagine how her hand would feel on his face. He placed his hand on hers. She turned her palm upward and lightly pressed his hand. Next to hers, his hand seemed strangely large and ruddy.

He moved closer to her. She carefully placed her drink on a small table before the couch, quietly announced she was becoming sleepy and placed her head on his shoulder. He put his arm around her and leaned his head against hers.

"Your hair tickles," he told her.

"Not unless you stick your nose into it," she said.

He stroked her cheek. "Your skin is soft," he whispered, "and kind of warm. You don't have a fever, do you?"

"Don't be funny, Mr. Perdue."

She slid out of his grasp, deftly but suddenly. "The smoke in this place is terrible and, for heaven's sake, everyone's staring at us!"

"I forgot where we were."

"Obviously." She got to her feet and took his hand. "Come on, let's get out of here."

"Where to?"

"My room. I *know* there's no one else there. That is, I *hope* not."

∞ ∞ ∞

The narrow road stretched before the wide windshield, curving around the edge of the mountain, overhanging the cliff. The lofty massiveness of the Adirondacks loomed before them and the valley fell away to the right of the road. The sky was clear blue and the mountain slopes were a budding, shy green. The spring air was gentle and slightly narcotic with its scent of new beginnings and of half-forgotten memories.

Ernie Waller occupied the driver's seat, his wide hands relaxed on the wheel, his pipe jutting from the corner of his mouth. He said, "Well, it doesn't seem like a half-year."

"Mmm, sure doesn't," Ed said.

"It ought to be a good weekend…especially if I find someone like ol' Flo."

"Oh, yes, I remember her. What was the story?"

"You know. She had her needs, same as I, she said, and no sense being cute about it. 'After all, this is 1957,' she said."

"Shy kid, huh?"

"Right. Hey, what happened with what's-her-name, the blonde?"

"Jean? Y'know, it's a funny thing."

"Will I laugh?"

Ed looked out the window. A few greyish clouds began to mar the clear sky. He turned back to Ernie and said, "After you and Florence left us, we started to warm up to each other. After a while, we went to her room for a little privacy."

"Mmm, I can imagine."

"Yeah, well I was imagining too, believe me. Anyway, since there was nothing else to sit on other than the bed, we sat on that."

"Sat?"

"Yes, sat. At first, anyway. Well, you know…it's not very relaxing sitting straight up. I mean, it's not like a chair or a couch or something with a back to it."

"What's all this background material? Cut the crap and get to the point."

"As I was saying, it wasn't very comfortable, so we sort of…"

"Relaxed?"

"Well…yes. And, *you* know, it was one thing leading to another. After a while, I thought sure 'this is it.'"

"You mean it wasn't?"
"No."
"After all that? How come?"
"We were both really carried away."
"Right."
"When it came down to..."
"Yeah, yeah. Go on."
"She started crying."
Ernie shot a look of deep disgust at his friend.
"Look, I'm telling you she started to cry. She gave me this routine about how she had never done "*that*" before, and how she couldn't live with herself if she did."
There was a moment of silence. Ernie stared ahead at the road, his lips pressed tightly together. Ed waited for a comment; finally, he broke the silence himself.
"Well, what do you think, Ernie?"
"You're asking for an opinion?"
"Well, yes."
"Look, Ed, so she said all that. They all say it; they have to say it so you don't think of them as some kind of...you know."
"I know what you mean, Ernie, but you had to *be* there. She wasn't just going through the expected motions."
Ed absently glanced out of the window. Past the white board fence on the side of the road was a sheer drop. Down below were rectangles of yellow and green and reddish-brown around tiny farmhouses. The mountains rose beyond. There were large, dark patches on the landscape where the rapidly-increasing clouds cast their shadows.
"Looks like rain," Ed commented. "We'd better get a move-on if we're going to stop by the construction site to see Dan Turner. That guy was some character."
"Listen, Ed. It *is* starting to look bad. Maybe we'd just better go straight to the lodge. The visibility might make for hard going later."
"C'mon, how bad can it be? We haven't seen that guy for six months, and it's practically on our way."
Ernie sighed. "Right. How bad can it be? Okay."
Twenty minutes later, they turned off the highway onto a dirt road that ran through the woods. The car bumped along at a crawl. Ernie said, "Better roll up the windows. It's starting to come down."
They soon arrived at a clearing in which there were some tents and trailers on the muddy ground. They stopped the car near a trailer bearing a hand-painted sign reading FOREMAN.

They stepped out of the car, turned up their jacket collars and sloshed through the mud to the trailer, their heads bowed to the rain. Ernie reached the door first, raised his hand to knock, hesitated and looked at Ed.

Ed yelled, "Hey, it's wet out here!" He pushed past Ernie and knocked on the door himself. They heard Dan's voice from inside, saying, "See who's there, will you, honey?"

"Does he have some broad living with him, Ernie?"

Ernie spat onto the muddy earth. The door opened. There was a blue bathrobe, ash-blonde hair and the astonished face of Jean.

THE ENIGMA OF REGINALD SAVAGE

Some startling, even fascinating, discoveries come one's way purely by chance at times. I was in Buenos Aires during July and August 1984 to interview the world-renowned writer, Jorge Luis Borges, and several other Argentine authors. One evening, I was a dinner guest at the elegant Arroyo Street apartment of the British-born playwright, William Shand. Among the guests were writers with whom I had been corresponding for years, but whom I had not met in person until that July. Julio Ricci, who had taken the boat from Montevideo to be present at this gathering, was involved in a heated discussion with Fernando Sorrentino. I joined them.

Ricci's round face was flushed. He turned to me and practically shouted, "Bah, you North Americans are prejudiced against Hispanic and other third-world peoples. You think we are inferior."

He was waving a sheaf of papers around as he spoke. Then he saw the look of surprise on my face, smiled and added, "I don't mean you, of course, Clark. After all, you are here because you appreciate our culture. I'm referring to a general attitude among your countrymen."

I started to protest when Sorrentino interrupted to explain that those papers Ricci had in his hand were the manuscript of a short story entitled, "Oil and Water," written by an American named Chuck Bradley.

"It's true, of course," said Sorrentino, "that this Chuck Bradley has a patronizing attitude toward Latin Americans, but he is only one writer. He represents no one but himself. "Besides," he added, turning to Ricci, "the term 'racist,' even applied to Bradley, would be a gross exaggeration."

Ricci pointed a finger at Sorrentino's face and opened his mouth to continue the argument, but I broke in. "Just who is Chuck Bradley and what kind of story is this?"

Sorrentino smiled and smoothed his moustache. He said, "Bradley can't be anyone of consequence. I never heard of him before."

"You want to know what kind of story it is?" sputtered Ricci.

"Here, take it." He grasped the manuscript by thumb and forefinger, stretched his arm full-length, wrinkled his nose as though he smelled something rotten and handed it to me. For a fraction of a second, I hesitated; I felt I was being offered a package of contamination.

More calmly, he added, "I'd like your opinion after you read it."

"It's in English," I foolishly observed.

Ricci raised an eyebrow. Sorrentino laughed. "The story's by an American. Americans do use English, I believe?"

Disregarding the sarcasm, I said, "Where did you get it, Julio?"

"I found it in the back of a locker at the New York Port Authority building, on my recent trip to the United States." He paused and added, "I see that you have never heard of this...this fellow. I'm glad to hear that, Zlotchew."

When I finally left the apartment, I took the manuscript (it was actually a carbon copy of a typescript, to be precise) to my less than elegant - I hate to say "cheap" - hotel in the Palermo district. The Hotel Panamé (yes, Panamé, not Panamá) was located on Calle Juan B. Justo near the Avenida Santa Fe. Since the management only supplied heat on request – typically in the morning and evening – I asked the desk clerk to pump some warm air into my room for the next hour (it was winter in the southern hemisphere). I sat up in bed to read "Oil and Water" before falling asleep.

On the back of the last page, I was able to distinguish "*feb. '52*" in tiny, penciled letters. The narrative turned out to be one of those typical adventure tales that appeared in "men's magazines" in the '50s and '60s. It contained a dash of sex, or rather, the mere *suggestion* of sex, which, in those relatively innocent times, would have been considered daring.

The action takes place in Venezuela, near the Brazilian and Colombian borders. The location is some fictitious oilfield at the headwaters of the Atabapo, one of the Amazon tributaries. The hero, Bob Johnson, refers condescendingly to the adjacent town, Santa Rosa, as a "tiny outpost of 'civilization,'" with "*civilization*" in quotation marks.

Johnson is a tall, lean, blonde, blue-eyed Texan: honest, decent, God-fearing and handy with his fists if the need arises. The villain, Pedro, is a pockmarked, swarthy, short but muscular Venezuelan. He is portrayed as sneaky, lecherous, treacherous and cruel. Pedro is unscrupulous and uses any means to get what he wants.

There is a beautiful Venezuelan girl, Pepita. A direct quotation from "Oil and Water" describing Johnson's first impressions of Pepita provides an idea of Chuck Bradley's style as well as his protagonist's attitude:

"Are you satisfy', or you wan' sometheen' else?"

This tangy-looking waitress in an off-the-shoulder peasant blouse showing lots of boob flashed her chocolaty eyes at me. Now, I've seen women in my time, but, man, this piece of Latin satin made my mouth hang open for a few seconds before I was able to concentrate enough on her question to finally come up with some kind of answer.

I said, "Well, yes, darlin', I surely do want somethin' else. What can you offer me?"

"Well, I got plenty..."

"I can see that."

"Don' be funny, Gringo. I mean the *bar* got plenty."

"Okay, honey. Make it another *aguardiente*."

"I be ri' back, Gringo." And she swung away like a pendulum in skirts.

∞ ∞ ∞

The laborers, according to the protagonist, "come from all over: Venezuela, Colombia, Brazil, Jamaica, Trinidad..." There is a group of Asians as well as a couple of Irishmen and some Italians too, and, according to the American, "who knows what-all." He then comments, "I've never seen so many different skin colors: white, black, brown, yellow and every shade in between." Then he informs the reader, "There's a lot of mixin' the races down there, you know."

In the local bar, the language he is able to distinguish, "out of all that babble," is mostly Spanish, "but there is some Portuguese, too, which is like a sloppy Spanish, and a few strange kinds of English, some you could hardly understand – like the Irish kind – and that sort of calypso English of the West Indian Negroes, and some weird clucking language that I guess is some kind of Indian lingo."

Pedro wants Pepita, but she (naturally) favors the American. Pedro is jealous of Pepita's attention to the Gringo and smacks her around, telling her that she belongs to him, Pedro. The chivalrous Texan unhesitatingly goes to her defense, and, in so doing, is obliged to fight. At one point in the brawl, the two men pause for breath, and Johnson good-naturedly tells Pedro they've both been drinking too much *aguardiente*, extends his hand and says, "Let's just forget about it and start all over."

Mistake. Pedro and the bloodthirsty saloon crowd take the Texan's good nature for cowardice. Pedro breaks a bottle and, after calling the hero - and, incidentally, all Americans - cowards, lunges for his opponent's face. Johnson parries the thrust and knocks Pedro unconscious. The local crowd, with the enthusiasm of a cockfight audience, screams, "*Mátalo, yanqui, mátalo*. Keel heem, Gringo. Feeneesh heem!"[1]

In revenge, Pedro arranges for the savage Chubacari Indians to capture Pepita. The American hires guides from the peaceful Chibcha tribe to take him by canoe to Chubacari country, but they drop him off short of that territory and flee in terror. With a machete, the intrepid narrator cuts his way through the dense jungle and, from the cover of trees, sees Pepita staked out in the center of the Chubacari village, naked. Standing over her, gloating, are two of the savages, naked as well but for multicolored beads around their necks, a knife hanging from a string around their waists and paint on their bodies. Johnson is shocked to see Pedro with them. For what ensues, I quote from "Oil and Water:"

> They stood over Pepita, and laughed and kind of taunted her. They babbled something to Pedro, and he answered in their savage lingo. Then he spoke to Pepita in Spanish. I could make out enough of what he was saying to know he was getting a charge out of filling her in on what to expect the next day. He seemed to be describing in detail the tortures they were going to subject her to. I couldn't get all of it, but judging by the expression on her face, it must have been pretty grim.
>
> Then he said something that made me want to run over and rip the son-of-a-bitch's guts out with my bare hands right then and there, but I controlled myself. He brought up the time she had said she wasn't like the other girls at the Bar La Gloria. He said, real slow and nasty, "So you don' crawl out of the woodwork, eh? Well, tomorrow you goin' to crawl." Then the bastard sort of giggled and went on. "*Sí*, you goin' to crawl *mañana*. You jus' wait on tables, eh? Nothing more than that, eh? An' you peeck your own friends? Well, tomorrow you goin' to do a lot more, an' weeth all *my* friends." He waved his arm to take in the whole village. "Sí, all my friends. And, of course, with me too. Ha! But don' worry, *chiquita*," and here his voice softened in mock tenderness, "you won' have to live long weeth the memory, jus' a few days…" Then he laughed a crazy, filthy laugh and the three men went back to the hut.

∞ ∞ ∞

Our hero waits for the village to sleep, cuts Pepita free, literally gives her the shirt off his back and flees with her through the jungle toward the Atabapo River. When they come to the river bank, they

---

[1] The demeaning imitation of English spoken with a Spanish accent is used throughout the story.

find a beached Chubacari war canoe and four warriors. The Texan manages to kill them all, get himself and Pepita into the canoe and paddle downstream while other war canoes pursue them.

They glide under tree branches marked by brightly colored feathers. At this point, the pursuers halt, since, as Pepita explains, the feathers mark the end of their territory, in which the gods are on the Chubacaris' side. Beyond this point, the Great Spirits of the Chubacari will not aid them. They see the Indians tie Pedro to a tree. Pepita explains this is because, having lost their intended victim, the savages believe the gods are with her and the American, but against Pedro.

After explaining this to the protagonist, "she gave a short laugh, a laugh that a little kid might let out when some grownup who's been bugging him falls down a flight of stairs." Johnson comments, "It bothered me." This, of course, would highlight American decency as opposed to foreign sadism. Then Pepita gleefully says, "Let's watch how they do eet...that dirty peeg. Let's watch!"

The Texan comments, "Well, damn, that was too much for me," and upbraids her for being so bloodthirsty. She gives him "a real mean look," and comments, "Aaayy...you Yanquis...soft hearts!" He clarifies, "And believe me, she didn't mean it as a compliment."

Johnson informs the reader that he and Pepita spent the next month in "pretty close company, if you get my drift," but in the end they realized they "weren't exactly the parts of the same jigsaw puzzle; we didn't fit too well. We were more like oil and water."

Johnson gives notice to the oil company and flies back to Houston via Caracas. The author has his narrator philosophically explain, "If two people have different ways of looking at life, it doesn't necessarily mean that one has the right way of looking at it and the other has the wrong way. That's not the way it is. It just means they're made of different stuff – like oil and water – and, like oil and water, they just can't mix, no matter how hard they try."

As I read it, I realized that, thinking of the attitude of everyone else in the story, this tolerant opinion on the part of the narrator actually flattered the American reader into thinking that we are all good people and that everyone else is evil. The Anglo-Saxon hero is so generous that he is even non-judgmental of those wicked and inferior people "down there."

I could see what Julio Ricci was so excited about. Of course, the story *could* be thought of as racist; however, American society in the '50s was very different from today's society, and we should probably take this into account in judging Chuck Bradley. Fernando Sorrentino, after all, believed Bradley was merely patronizing rather than frankly racist. More to the point, I thought Ricci was wrong in saying that Bradley's perspective reflected the attitude of Americans today.

Curiously, the matter did not end with my reading the story in Buenos Aires. There were fascinating repercussions several months later.

∞ ∞ ∞

One Friday afternoon of the fall semester of 1984, I was in downtown Fredonia. I was having a beer at the White Inn's Friday Happy Hour with Dave Lunde, the college writer-in-residence at the time. We were talking about American science fiction, or rather, *he* was talking about American science fiction; I was half-heartedly listening, my mind wandering somewhere out there in Argentina. Suddenly, something he said snapped me out of my reverie.

"Who?" I interrupted.

"What...? Oh, that was Reginald Savage. Why?"

"No, no. The other name."

Dave narrowed his eyes, slowly shook his head and smiled. "How many beers did you say you had before I got here?" He sounded somewhat snide.

"C'mon, c'mon. The other name...?"

Dave impatiently fingered the curled tips of his Salvador Dalí-style moustache and sighed. "I was saying that Reginald Savage, one of the finest science fiction writers of the 1950s, sometimes wrote stories for some of the so-called men's magazines under the pseudonym Chuck Bradley, and that..."

"That's what I thought you said!"

"Yes. Well?"

"Chuck Bradley's real name was Reginald Savage?"

"Apparently."

"Why did he use a pen name?"

Dave chuckled. "You ever read any of those Bradley stories?"

"Yes, as a matter of fact."

"Which one?"

"Something called 'Oil and Water.'"

"I think I read it, too," Dave said, "just out of curiosity. It was in one of those magazines with men's adventure stories and lots of pictures of half-naked women. You interested in Savage?"

"In Bradley."

"Same thing. Look, get over to the Reed Library at the college. Gerda Morrissey will help you dig up some information on Savage, or Bradley, or whatever-the-heck you want to call him."

∞ ∞ ∞

Not only did Gerda Morrissey show me where to find a great deal of information in the Reed Library on Reginald Savage (alias Chuck Bradley), she told me that the library of the University of Texas-at-Austin had a Savage Collection, including letters written by Savage to friends, colleagues and publishers. The collection also included letters written to him. I flew to Austin during my winter break to study that correspondence. Several of the handwritten letters shed light on the writing of "Oil and Water," the question of the alias and the personality of the man. For example:

December 18, 1951
Dear (name illegible),
As you know, I'm really getting discouraged. Have been depressed for some time now, actually. I like my science fiction; I think it's good. "Naturally," you're probably saying. But you like it too, and some other friends like it (but are they unprejudiced?). Still, the magazine publishers don't like it; in fact, they think it's garbage, to put it politely. I keep getting rejection slips, most without the courtesy of a personalized comment. The few editors who do take the trouble to comment refer to "unbelievability," or dependence on "gimmicks," or a "lack of humanity," etc. You know. Anyway, while I'm waiting for their time to come, I've decided to write the kind of stories I know I can get published and get paid for. You won't like the stories very much (neither will I). In fact, I won't even use my real name in the byline on this crap. But, give the public what it wants, they say. Right?

The rest of this letter is inconsequential. In a letter of January 4, 1952, sent to someone addressed as "Querida Peggy,"[2] Savage says:

I've been very scientific about it, made a thorough study of the market. I feel I could successfully write for the "men's magazines," like the publications controlled by United Magazine Service, Inc., especially the one called *Hero*, which has wide readership in the states of Texas, Oklahoma and Colorado. Now, what does its wide readership in those states tell you? It tells me that a substantial proportion of the readership has connections with the petroleum industry. I believe that most of the readers probably have worked - or contemplate working - in overseas oil fields as well as in domestic ones.

Savage goes on to explain to Peggy that he felt it would be easier to situate the action of his story in Venezuela because the prospective readers, even if they had worked in that country, would

2   "querida" is Spanish for "dear" (f.). I wondered why Savage would use Spanish.

not be sufficiently familiar with local customs to be in a position to say that his writing was "phony." It would have been difficult for him to have placed the action in Texas, for example, because Savage (or Bradley) knew nothing of conditions in those oil fields and in neighboring towns, whereas the readers probably did. Under those circumstances, he writes, Venezuela, paradoxically, was easier for him to write about, *even though he had never been there*, than writing about Texas or Oklahoma or Colorado.

He knew neither Venezuela nor those Western states, but he knew more about Venezuela (through reading) than his readers would, or so he thought. But he definitely knew much less than his readers about those Western states.

Still, he placed an additional safeguard in the story, and here he evinces considerable pride in his shrewdness: he situated the action in some spurious oil fields in the southern part of the country at the headwaters of the Amazon tributaries, rather than in the well-known fields of Lake Maracaibo in the North. After all, he reasoned, some readers would undoubtedly have worked in the Maracaibo fields and would have realized that the writer had no familiarity with them.

In his letter of February 2, 1952, to Jack Perloff, one of the Beat Generation poets, Savage admits, with a definite sense of guilt, or shame, that in "Oil and Water" he appealed to the sensibilities of men he believed to be like many of the regular Navy men he had encountered during his time in the Service, especially those from the Southern states. The hero would, therefore, be the archetypal American: white, Anglo-Saxon and Protestant. This WASP would also be superior physically, mentally and morally to the surrounding Venezuelans. In this way, Savage calculated, the average reader of *Hero* would identify with the protagonist and would be rewarded with "a feeling of superiority" while reading the story.

"People want to be entertained," he writes, "and most people are entertained by being spectators at readily understood, very physical activities, especially those that are appreciated visually. This is why," he continues, "football and baseball – sports in general – are so popular. And movies, especially those with huge doses of sex and violence. In other words," he says, "most people don't want to have to think; they would rather sit back and be stimulated on the instinctual level by vicarious thrills." He adds, "But they also *love* to be flattered, to be made to feel superior, and 'Oil and Water' does that too."

Apparently, Savage's homework was worth the effort; the story appeared in *Hero*, and, in Savage's own words, he received a "healthy check," which represented not only material gain for him, but he confesses, satisfied his ego in the same manner in which the story was designed to satisfy the ego of the reader. It was a "pat on the back for a job well done," he writes, the job being that of satisfying the reading public - or, at least a large segment of it - rather than self-indulgently catering to his own artistic needs.

In this letter, he metaphorically employs the term "coitus" to represent the artist's satisfaction of the public's needs, of "stroking" the public, as we might say today, as opposed to the "masturbation" of indulging in the satisfaction of his own artistic sensibilities. (These references to eroticism lead me to wonder if the term *prostitution* might be more accurate than mere *coitus*, considering that Savage performed the artistic act for financial gain rather than out of love. But that is neither here nor there.)

Another letter is especially interesting to me because it deals with a linguistic problem. The letter, dated February 14, 1952, is addressed to Professor A. Bolognesi of Harpur College.[3]

In it, Savage refers to "Getting the Message," an unpublished story of his, a story he obviously considers far superior to "Oil and Water." In this unpublished story, which takes place in some mythical Central American republic, he employs a correct and restrained diction, a rather formal English, a language intended to suggest that the personages are speaking Spanish – their own tongue – rather than broken English.[4]

On the other hand, the Venezuelans of "Oil and Water" speak English with Spanish accents. This accent was made broadly obvious, he relates, almost a burlesque, in "sight dialect."[5] And, he points out, the "mishandling of English, always considered an indication of stupidity by those [English speakers] who really are not highly intelligent themselves,"[6] would aid in providing a feeling of superiority for the reader whose English presumably was perfect – "perfectly native, that is."

The reader, Savage was convinced, would not trouble himself to reflect that his inability to speak the language of his host country - be it Venezuela, Saudi Arabia or anywhere else - might represent a lack in his own character. Nor would it occur to him that the fluent - even if mispronounced - English of the natives might represent an enviable achievement.

    3   Now part of the State University of New York at Binghamton

    4   The reader will have noticed a certain propensity on the part of Bradley/Savage to situate his fiction in Latin America. This is significant.

    5   E.g., writing "keel heem" for "kill him," or "I be ri' back" for "I'll be right back."

    6   This statement could be ambiguous, but, from context, it is clear that Savage did not mean to insinuate that all English speakers are unintelligent, an obviously indefensible position, but that he was referring exclusively to those English speakers (whose name is legion) who think this way.

In short, Savage read the temper of the time and place, wrote for a specific readership and, therefore, experienced success. In his letters, it emerges that he was proud of this accomplishment and congratulated himself on having provided pleasure – "real entertainment value" – for others.

"Oil and Water," of course, was only the first of a series of similar stories published by *Hero* and comparable magazines. These stories, under the pseudonym Chuck Bradley, were his mainstay until his science fiction finally became widely accepted. Then he became famous, under what I presumed was his real name – Reginald Savage – as well as rich, on the basis of his science fiction.

Something disturbed me: He repeatedly claims feeling pride in writing and selling "Oil and Water," and similar stories (and personally, I feel they are valuable documents testifying to the times), yet, his byline was a *pseudonym*! If he was proud of those stories, why did he sign them with the name Chuck Bradley? Obviously, he did not want to be known as the author of those works; he merely wanted to receive his checks.

The foregoing, fascinating though it may be, pales in comparison with the startling facts I am about to relate. The full extent of his shame at being the author of "Oil and Water" became known to me in late June, 1985.

I presented a paper, "Borges, Omar and Amoral Fiction," at the Symposium on Borges/With Borges held at Allegheny College in Meadville, Pennsylvania. Jorge Luis Borges was present throughout the four-day event, and, to my great surprise, he remembered me from our interview in Buenos Aires the year before. I had the opportunity to speak with him at length during the symposium. One evening over dinner, Borges astounded me by referring to, and I quote literally, "the great American science fiction writer": Reginald Savage!! He went on at great length about Savage's fertile imagination and his economical use of language.

Apparently, many of Savage's works had been translated into Spanish; however, Borges had read every single story of Savage's in the original English. In spite of this, he was totally unaware of the work (and even the existence) of Chuck Bradley. Consequently, I was astonished when Borges stated, in an off-handed manner, "You know, of course, Reginald Savage was not his real name."

Without a pause (being blind, he could not have noticed the expression of amazement on my face), Borges continued, "He was one of us, of course. Did you know that?"

Receiving no immediate reaction from me (I was too stunned to speak for several seconds), Borges looked puzzled. He seemed to be waiting for some sign of life on my part. Finally, he asked, "Zlotchew, are you there?"

I managed to stammer, "One of *you*...?"

"Yes. I mean, he was Hispanic, or Latino, or whatever the fashionable term is these days. But, didn't you know that?"

It took me a moment to digest this data.

"Hispanic?! No...I didn't."

"Oh, yes, of course. His real name was Nelson Rivera. Curious name for a Hispanic: Nelson. But I'm told it's popular in Puerto Rico."

"He was Puerto Rican?"

"Well, he was born in Jersey City, I believe, but his mother was Puerto Rican and his father was from Spain – a *gallego*, as we call them – via Cuba.[7] He took me to meet his mother on one occasion – in 1959 or 1960, I believe. His father had died many years before.

"Savage, or Rivera," Borges continued, "had been drinking a great deal one evening. I distinctly recall the pungent aroma of rum. We were discussing the science fiction genre, and that's when he told me of his origins."

"But...why on earth had he changed his name?"

"Commercial reasons." Borges paused. "You must remember how it was absolutely necessary - in the '30s, the '40s and part of the '50s - for Hollywood stars and other entertainment figures to have Anglo-Saxon names, in order to be accepted by the masses. Or at least that's what the Hollywood moguls thought."

"Yes, that's true."

"Of course. For example, do you remember Gilbert Roland?"

"Sure. He was a leading man back in the '40s."

"Actually, he started playing leading men in the silent films of the 1920s - I'm a film buff, you know - and acted in dozens of films right down to 1979 or 1980."

"All right, but what's that got to do with...?"

"Do you know his real name, or where he was born?"

"I have no idea."

He was born in Mexico: either in Juárez or Chihuahua, I don't remember which. His real name was Luis Antonio Dámaso de Alonso. They wouldn't accept a mouthful like that in Hollywood, so he changed it to Gilbert Roland. Much easier, no?" He chuckled.

"But there were actors with Spanish names..."

"Yes, Ramón Novarro, Lupe Vélez, Leo Carrillo, César Romero... but they were restricted to playing Hispanics or other 'exotics.'

---

7 Literally, "gallego" means "Galician," i.e. that is, from Galicia, a region in the extreme northwest of Spain. The term is loosely used by Latin Americans in colloquial speech to refer to Spaniards in general.

You know, moustached Latin lovers or criminals or bullfighters, or their female counterparts: hot-tempered, wildly passionate 'spitfires' named Pepita or Rosita. This strictly limited their careers while promoting the ridiculous stereotype."

Borges paused for a moment. "And there were all those Jewish immigrants or their children: Bernie Schwartz, whom we know as Tony Curtis; Edward G. Robinson, who had been born Emmanuel Goldenberg in Rumania; Danny Kaye, born David Kaminsky; John Garfield, born Julius Garfinkle; Kirk Douglas, born Issur Danielovitch."

I was fascinated. Borges thought for a moment and then smiled. "And then there was Rita Hayworth. Ah, yes, Rita Hayworth..." A dreamy expression passed across his features, softening the lines of his face. He paused for a moment. "Rita, one could say, was of both Jewish and Hispanic extraction; her real family name was Cansinos, you know, of Sephardic origin, like the great Spanish poet Cansinos-Assens."

With this, Borges pounded his cane against the floor, as though indicating he was returning to the subject. "Anyway," he said, "they were all changing their names. The whole phenomenon is quite astonishing, seen from our vantage point in the present, no?"

"Yes," I said, "but it's not like that now."

"Mercifully, no. All that has changed, of course, and I think it was already changing back in the '50s. Although, more recently, there's the case of that actor, what's his name...Martin Sheen, that's it. Yes, Martin Sheen. They tell me he is, or has been, very popular. I'm told his real name is Ramón Estévez. You know? Still, Rivera had *legally* changed his name to Savage back in the '40s."

I was dumbfounded. Borges faced me for what seemed an eternity, no doubt waiting for some reaction on my part. Finally, thinking either that I had left the table or that I was some kind of imbecile posing as an academic, he shrugged and turned to María Kodama and began to speak to her about some book they were preparing together concerning Japan.

I have not been able to find any written evidence anywhere of Reginald Savage's Latino background; nevertheless, there is a record, in the Jersey City Registry, of a Nelson Rivera having been born in 1922. However, Nelson is a fairly common name among Puerto Ricans, and Rivera is as common a surname among them as Smith is in the U.S. There are also records of a Nelson Rivera attending school from kindergarten through graduation from Ferris High School in 1940. I didn't attempt to trace his name any further. Savage, of course, has often referred to his experiences with the Navy in World

War II, but I don't know if he served officially under the name Rivera or Savage.

Personally, I don't think "Oil and Water" and those other stories under the byline Chuck Bradley are so terrible. They are good examples of adventure fiction. Certainly, they did show the hero as superior to the other characters, but the hero is the hero, after all. And, if the story takes place in foreign locales, the other characters are going to be foreigners, naturally. Of course, the result is that the American hero, being the hero, is portrayed as superior to others. And since this American is, in addition, a WASP, all other races seem to be depicted as inferior. This could produce the impression that the author was a racist. Of course, he wasn't, was he?

I could be wrong, but I think Julio Ricci overreacted. Savage himself, or Chuck Bradley, or Nelson Rivera, overreacted, obviously, when you think of how he died in 1976 at the age of 54: In his Manhattan condominium, from a lethal combination of alcohol and barbiturates.* He must have been despondent. He must have been feeling some sense of guilt, of having betrayed his origins, perhaps.

* Editor's note: Dr. Zlotchew is mistaken. While the death he describes is "common knowledge," i.e., most people accept it as the truth, it is a myth. The fact is that Reginald Savage died on March 3, 1977, in a hospital in San Carlos de Río Negro, Venezuela, at the headwaters of the Amazon tributaries, from injuries sustained in an altercation with a laborer over a woman in the TexVenCo oilfields located 21 kilometers south of San Carlos de Río Negro. Viz. obituary in The New York Times, March 8, 1977, and in El Noticiero of Caracas, March 5, 1977.

FEAR OF FAILURE

Yes, doctor, I was considered exceptionally beautiful when I was in high school, as I still am. Well, that's obvious, of course. You're looking right at me. Yet, believe it or not, I wasn't really popular. *Popular*, that's the word. It was very important for a girl to be popular. You see, the boys my own age were afraid to attempt any friendship with me. In fact, most simply avoided me. I understood later that they were terrified, absolutely terrified. They feared rejection and they assumed that a girl as beautiful, and intelligent as I was, would be unattainable. As a result, I simply was not...*attained* by anyone, during the first two years of high school.

Most of the girls weren't very friendly, either. Doubtless, they were jealous of me, of my beauty and charm. I am quite charming, you know. I'm telling you this because I realize that, under the present circumstances - in your professional capacity, so to speak - you might not be fully aware of this. You and I are not in a, shall we say, social situation. At any rate, I had very few girl friends. There was only one real friend all through the four years of high school. She was beautiful, just as I was, but Gina wasn't quite as *intellectual* as I was.

Far from it, in fact.

She managed to have boyfriends, though. I don't know... Only one or two had the nerve to approach her, but the one or two...oh, let's be honest, there were at least five of them and they were all attractive. They were athletes, and they were intelligent and had good senses of humor and, of course, they were aggressive. They were older than she, a year or two ahead of her in school. What? No, I was not jealous of her. Well, maybe I was. Just a tiny bit. I mean, we have to tell the truth, the absolute truth here, don't we? Even if it hurts. Or else, what's the use of coming here and spending scads and scads of money? I don't wish to be crude, doctor, but you know as well as I that you charge an arm and a leg. Yes, I know my husband doesn't do his work out of humanitarian zeal, either, but you just sit there and listen to people. No, no! I'm not feeling hostile today. I'm just stating a fact.

To get back to me - that *is* why I'm putting my husband's hard-earned cash into your well-lined pockets, isn't it, now? To get back to me, I was somewhat...envious...of Gina. She was beautiful, as I was...as I *am*...but she was beautiful in rather a, shall we say, *coarse*, manner. She was a straight C student, if you catch my drift, and I was straight A. That's another reason boys were afraid of me, and why quite a few girls avoided me too, as a matter of fact. Still, she was the only real friend I had in high school.

The teachers liked me, I'll say that, especially the male teachers. They recognized my special qualities. And whereas the female teachers often tempered their admiration of my intellectual prowess with resentment for my beauty - it was only natural, I suppose - the males didn't suffer from any such problem. On the contrary, doctor, on the contrary.

But my rapport with the teachers is most likely the reason I was given the part of Carmen in the senior play. I mean, I certainly looked the part, of course. That is, I'm beautiful and dark, like Carmen. And I am a wonderful actress. Really. Everyone told me so. You see, the thing is, I'd have to be a great actress in order to play the part of Carmen. After all, I'm not exactly what you would call *primitive*. I'm not *tempestuous*. I mean, I'm not the sort of person who is governed by her passions, which is the sort of person Carmen was. But, of course, one doesn't have to be the kind of person one is portraying if one is truly an actor or actress. Actually, if they had wanted to do typecasting, they would have done better with Gina. Perhaps that sounds catty. No, no...I say it with all sincerity. I'm being frank; that's just the way she was. That's the only reason I'm mentioning it - really.

At any rate, coming back to me, there were all these absolute babies, these callow, unsophisticated, immature babies...people like Ed Perdue, skinny as a rail, horn-rimmed glasses...the classic nerd. And that muscle-bound, airheaded football player, Clarence Mahoney; he liked to be called *Rhino*. Have you ever heard of someone who actually *wanted* to be compared to an animal? And Sal Puglisi; he thought he was some kind of Don Juan, always looking in mirrors, even his reflection in windows, combing his dark hair... always being too familiar with all the girls. At least *he* had the good sense to *pretend* I didn't interest him. And all those others, always ogling me, looking dreamily at me and sighing, hanging around at a distance, if you know what I mean. No, no, it's not really a paradox, but you've got to picture what I mean. You see, they would hang around me at a *distance*. That is, they would manage to sit about four seats away from me – no further, but no closer either – because they were ashamed, as well they might be. Just imagine, those little babies, those nothings, interested in a person as beautiful, as intelligent, as charming and as accomplished as I!

Well, yes, I know it's hard for you to believe they could even *consider*, in their wildest *dreams*, my dear, that I... Well, in short, there was no one suitable, not even in the upper grades. Look here, you don't know Snyder High. It's an absolute wasteland, an intellectual desert, I assure you.

At any rate, the teachers were rather taken with me, especially the male teachers. And something rather interesting happened when I was a junior. Mr. Goldfarb, my biology instructor, kept me after school one day. I was totally mystified, totally. I mean, I couldn't *imagine* what was wrong. I was a good student in biology and it was obvious to me that Mr. Goldfarb liked me, so I couldn't imagine why he asked me to stay after school.

Well, you see, it turned out that he was "hot for me," as they colloquially and crudely, I might add, say nowadays. I mean, he found me sexually attractive. But then, everyone did. I mean, if they were males. Come to think of it, not necessarily only males, but that's beside the point. What...? Maybe it isn't, you say? Whatever do you...? Well, at least let me finish my story about my biology teacher. You see, Mr. Goldfarb also appreciated my intellectual qualities, of course. I say "of course" because he was a sensitive and intelligent person in addition to being a man. I mean, he didn't say anything about finding me sexually desirable. Naturally, the poor man - he was 32 years old - wouldn't come out and say that to a 17-year-old student of his. I mean, I'm sure he wanted to keep his job and I'm sure he must have known about statutory rape...

I liked him too. He was so...so mature and intelligent, and thoughtful and sensitive, and so...well, *mature*. Not like those drooling, disgusting, horrible high school beasts with their pimples and dandruff and halitosis and the constant smell of perspiration, who could think of only one thing... What? *What was that one thing,* you say? Really, doctor, you know exactly what I mean. You must have been one of those creepy adolescents at one time, too. Well, if you really have no imagination, or, more to the point, you get some kind of thrill hearing your female patients being very specific, talking dirty, as they say... I mean, they were interested only in...slaking their sexual thirst on any female foolish enough to allow them near her. What? Oh, yes, I said *any* female, and I meant it. Some females drew them more than others, of course, like myself, for reasons I've already explained.

I just didn't appreciate their attentions, unlike some people. I mean, you should have seen that slut of a drum majorette from Ferris

High – Patricia Hanley or Hamlet or Hanlon or something – prancing and cavorting, showing everything she had, enjoying - absolutely *delighting!* - in the way those pathetic hormone-driven adolescent high school boys were gawking and drooling... Simply *exulting* in it. She actually relocated, after graduation, to Los Angeles. She was hoping to do great things in Hollywood. What? Well, yes, I went out there, too, and I did very well. I had connections there. I have relatives in L.A., and they were acquainted socially with the brilliant British director, Peter Cox, who has been working in Hollywood for years now. Besides, I'm a very talented actress. Everyone told me that in high school, and in Hollywood. And, you know, my dear, it is not sufficient to have acting talent and beauty. I put myself in Peter's hands and let him mold me. Under Mr. Cox's tutelage I learned how to use my God-given charisma to charm the audiences, to "grab them by the lapels," as Petey used to say, and make them love me. No doubt you've seen me starring in 'Knight Errant.'

Oh, you haven't? I am truly shocked, my dear man! It was a breathtakingly superb film, and I was magnificent as the star. Doctor, you really should get out more. What? So, why am I not still out there making movies? Well, I became bored with all that glitz and glamour. I had my years of glory and now I'm happy with married life. What? If I'm so happy, why do I come here? Yes, all right; I'll have to think about that, but I seem to have gotten off the subject.

At any rate he, Mr. Goldfarb, told me he was keeping me after school because I was so exceptionally intelligent and did so well in biology that he thought that, with a little guidance, I could attain perfection. One would have to have been an utter fool not to notice the way he was gazing at me as he spoke. He'd lean over my desk, about an inch from my face. He smelled so masculine: "Plaid" after-shave, I believe, and some kind of spearmint drops. He leaned over my desk and breathed in my ear. Well, of course he'd be giving me some kind of instruction or answering some question of mine, but he'd get real close and would be breathing in my ear.

His eyes were so intense and searching. Yes, he would gaze into my eyes in a manner I can only describe as *searching*, as though he wished to penetrate my very *soul*. And he swept his eyes along my long dark tresses. What? My *hair*, doctor, my *hair*. And over my smooth, bare arms and my neck and my firm, generous breasts. It gives me gooseflesh to think of it, even now. Well, who could blame the poor man? Just because he was married and had a little girl didn't make him any less *human*, now did it? I mean, really…

At any rate, up to that point I had been receiving "B"s in biology when I really would have liked to - I really *deserved* to – receive "A"s.

It's just that he was a most demanding instructor. I thought, if I play my cards right and take advantage of his obvious admiration for me, perhaps I would be able to receive an "A" in the end. Pardon me...? Oh, yes, I suppose that was an unfortunate construction. But let's not use my valuable time here for facetiousness. Now, let's get back to my grades. I mean, there's such a thin line between a "B," if it's a high "B," and a low "A." Sometimes it's just a question of whether the teacher was feeling well when he was correcting your test or whether he had a headache. Sometimes it's directly on the borderline, and if you had spoken to him in an insolent manner that day, he'd push you down to a "B," whereas, if you had smiled at him, he would raise it to an "A." That's the way the world is, you know. You have to have a little sophistication if you want to succeed in this world. Yes, success is important, very important.

    At any rate, he worked on me, I mean, *with* me, three times after school, but I was still getting "B"s on quizzes. The third time, after he gave back the quiz taken during the third after-school session, I suggested my going to his place. You see, I remembered he had mentioned earlier, in class, that his wife and little child were visiting his in-laws in Detroit for a couple of weeks. I suggested it because I thought it would be more conducive to accomplishing things.

    Well, I tell you, my dear, his face turned red, absolutely beet red, which would be a strange reaction to a student's suggestion for getting something accomplished, don't you think? And he began to pant. I mean that quite literally. He actually started to pant, my dear. That's the only word for it, I assure you. My God, the poor man was staring at my lips, my breasts, my lap...and he was *panting*, for God's sake!

    To get back to the story, I went to his house the following day at precisely 3:30 and, at 5:30, I left as a woman. I mean to say, I went in as a mere girl, but I emerged a full-fledged woman. You know what I mean. And he was so sweet. The poor man had cold hands and was stuttering and shaking...I mean, he was actually trembling like a leaf. But his hands finally warmed up and he did things to me I had never even imagined. I assure you, he was beside himself.

    What...? What *kinds* of things did he do? Oh, come now, doctor, surely you have an imagination. Surely, you don't want me to enumerate all the intimate little details, do you? You do? You know, I'm really beginning to wonder about you people. I mean, everyone says you're merely highly-paid voyeurs. Or perhaps it would be more accurate to say *écouteurs* or *auditeurs*. You *do* understand French, don't you? Anyone with any claim to being civilized, my dear man, should be able to speak French. I mean, my goodness! But I digress... What? No, not *trans*gress- *di*gress.

Back to Mr. Goldfarb. You do have an imagination, don't you? Look at me, just look at me. I'm a beautiful woman. I was 17 then. Can you imagine? Doctor...? Doctor? Oh, come on now, snap out of it. Yoohoo, doctor, come back to earth. Oh, your mind wandered for just a moment. Well, it's not supposed to. Not at these rates. Yes, well, he simply worshipped me. Mr. Goldfarb, of course. He adored me. I mean, in the most literal sense. Do you understand what I'm saying, doctor?"

∞ ∞ ∞

"Well, doctor, here I am again. Another 45 minutes, another bag of gold for your coffers. Isn't that so? What? It's 50 minutes, you say? Well... No, no, I'm not being hostile. At any rate, as I started to tell you last time, before you so unfeelingly cut me off, in my senior year, my parents were becoming somewhat concerned about me. No girl friends except for Gina. No boyfriends. And they thought my friendship with Mr. Goldfarb was just a tad excessive between a girl my age - a high school student - and a married man with a child.

I had assured them, naturally, that their fears were unfounded, that our friendship was purely platonic and intellectual. Nevertheless, they thought it was just not *healthy*. That was the word they used. It was not healthy to pursue a relationship of that nature any further. If only they were aware of precisely what nature it actually was. My mother seemed worried, but a bit wistful too. My father seemed worried and just a wee bit enraged. To come to the point, they introduced me to this young medical student, Ronald Sturgess, the son of a friend of my father's, and we started to date.

He came from a very good family, was fairly attractive, was doing well in his studies, was kind and considerate, and would soon be making scads and scads of money. He certainly was all of that, but he was not what you would call *ardent*. We hit it off well and, to make a long story short, we were married after two years of dating and one year of engagement, during which time Ron was a perfect gentleman, I assure you. I was flattered that he never laid a hand on me; I thought it showed that he respected me and that he loved me for reasons that went beyond the merely physical attraction I simply knew had to exist, given my great beauty. I mean, everyone, simply everyone, thought I was a great beauty.

We went to Mexico City and Acapulco for our honeymoon, and that's where I... It was a terrible shock, doctor, to find... I'm sorry, forgive me. I really didn't intend to cry, to lose control like this. Just give me a moment, just one moment. Thank you...

He kept telling me his back was bothering him. Well, all right, I could understand that. However, to tell me that he didn't want to kiss me because he was getting a virus? We called it the 'grippe' back then. That was excessive, I felt. And then, when I found him at one o'clock in the morning helping Ramón clean out the swimming pool...that's what he said they were doing - cleaning the swimming pool. It was more than I could bear. I mean, can you just imagine? I came down to look for him and I found him behind a palm tree, at one in the morning, on our *honeymoon*, for God's sake! He was with an *employee*, for God's sake, of the damned *hotel*! They were stark naked, cleaning out the pool! I could have killed him! Can you just *imagine* the scene? He had the effrontery to try and tell me that he was helping Ramón clean the fucking pool! Oh! Forgive me, doctor. That's not me. I don't talk that way. I'm really sorry. Yes, I know it's perfectly normal to get this angry, this upset, but it's not normal for *me*. What? You think that maybe it would be better for me if it *were* normal? Oh, come now, doctor. Yes, I know you're perfectly serious, but… Yes, another Kleenex, please. Thank you. Just give me a moment. Oh, God!

    Now, the problem, you see, is that to me, marriage is sacred, for better or worse. It's a sacrament, and not to be dismissed lightly. Of course, it was never consummated, that's true, so I could have had the marriage anulled; I still could. But I'm not going to. What would my parents think, my whole family? How could I explain that I had… That I had…*failed*! I, Lana Swank, had failed. All my friends would find out. What do you mean, "*what* friends?" Oh, yes. Of course. I've got to remember to let my defenses down while I'm in this office.

    Well, everyone I had gone to school with would find out. They would know that I, Lana Swank, had failed at marriage. In my family, the worst sin is failure. How could I ever face them again? How could I ever go to a class reunion? And not just them…all Jersey City, all New Jersey, everyone who counted in New Jersey, would know. So would my relatives in New York and Los Angeles and Birmingham. I'd be a laughing stock! It would be a terrible joke and I would be the butt of it.

    Besides, Ron is very rich and I have everything I need, everything I could ever imagine in my wildest dreams. What, doctor? Except happiness? Well, who's to say what happiness consists of? I'm comfortable. I'm married to a highly-respected and successful gynecologist, who also happens to be a kind, considerate, intelligent man. Yes, of course, and exceedingly wealthy. We all have our little peculiarities, our foibles, after all. God knows what *you* do in your private life, doctor…

    At any rate, we came to an accommodation. You see, he doesn't want his parents to know his…situation, either. And he doesn't believe in divorce unless there is no other way out. He didn't want his colleagues to know; he'd be disgraced, ruined. I mean, this is America. It's the middle of the 20th century. This is not Ancient Greece where all those philosophers liked to play with little boys and it was considered quite the thing to do. I mean, it just isn't the thing to do in our culture. Not yet, at any rate.

Well then, we agreed that he would have his friends, and I would have mine. The only trouble is that I feel very strongly - *very* strongly - about the Ten Commandments. "Thou shalt not commit adultery," you know. So, as long as I remain married to Ron, I absolutely will not, could not, bring myself to let any other man's penis penetrate my vagina. What? What about Peter Cox, you say, and Mr. Goldfarb? But I wasn't married at that time. It wasn't adultery. Now, however, I *am* married. I know it sounds irrational in this day and age, in view of the situation, but my feelings are very strong on this matter. You're always telling me to get in touch with my feelings, aren't you? Yes, well, those are my feelings.

I mean, both Ron and you could give me written permission... even the president of the United States, even the Pope - well, I know the Pope wouldn't give me permission, but even my *father*, for God's sake...and I still couldn't do it. My vagina is the portal to the sacred vessel and I am the keeper of the keys. That's the way I feel. Well, yes, doctor, I'm open-minded. We can investigate it further. Yes, I'll try to really get in touch with my feelings. But, you see... Oh? So soon? But how can you be so heartless? All you ever think about is the time, because "time is money," isn't it? Can't you ever be human? Yes, I know someone else is waiting to see you and you have to help him or her, too. It's just that. Oh, all right doctor. Next week...

GOING FOR THE GOLD

He sat sprawled on his stained and tattered easy-chair, a six-pack of Budweiser at his feet, one of the bottles in his left hand, the remote in his right. He took a long gulp of beer, laid the remote down next to the pink teddy bear on the metal tray table before him and reached for the Big Mac. He closed his eyes and savored the succulent beef patties, the cheese, the lettuce, onion, pickles, sesame bun, and the secret recipe "special sauce" that Joe Sims was sure contained mayo, ketchup and relish. He let his taste buds bathe in the savory juices as his teeth and tongue caressed the food before he gulped the mass down. He felt its bulk pass satisfyingly all the way to his stomach where it came to rest, producing a feeling of contentment. The contentment faded when he looked at the pink teddy bear. He sighed deeply, then tore his eyes from the stuffed animal.

Joe Sims had just returned from the Lakeland Ice Cream Factory to an empty house. He had sweated the day away on the production line in 100-degree heat, yet his hands froze numb while packing those ice pops as fast as he could so his supervisor wouldn't yell at him. *In fire and ice,* he thought. *All that's missing is the devil jabbing my ass with a pitchfork.* He felt shame and rage when Mr. Hanson, in front of his co-workers, called him a lazy slug, just like his father used to do. Except his father would smack him around, too, and later tell him it was for his own good, because he loved him. Joe would have dearly enjoyed smashing Hanson's round, pink face into mush, but he needed the job.

He took another slug of the Bud from this, his third bottle. *The first is for the thirst, the second one to make sure, the third is to relax...* He felt the bitter effervescence change to sweetness on his tongue, the cold liquid in his mouth to a soothing warmth in his belly. He told himself he felt good. *Good food, good drink and the Olympics on the little screen. Eat, drink and make merry. Or is it Mary? What more could you ask for?* He belched contentedly. He unbuckled his belt and unzipped his fly, to give himself breathing space. Hell, in high school he had to put extra holes in his belt so his pants wouldn't fall down. He still had the muscles, he reassured himself, they just weren't quite as hard as they used to be. But he could get back into shape easily, whenever he wanted.

The men on the T.V. screen were frying fresh-caught fish, drinking beer and smiling ecstatically at each other. *Damn commercial. Now, what brand is it? Ah, who gives a flying…? Beer is beer. Screw those fat cats on Madison Avenue. Look at that: those good old boys seem to be having a great time just sitting around, eating, drinking and grinning at each other like assholes.* "It just doesn't get any better than this," one of them said. *What the hell do they know? Bunch of faggots, probably.* He tossed the empty bottle onto the floor – one more dead soldier – and reached for the fourth bottle. *The fourth is for…damn, I can't remember what the hell it is for. The fourth is…to relax even more.* He twisted the cap off, skinning his finger, and took a long swallow.

On the screen, the runners were burning up the track. God, he felt good watching them run, as though he were watching himself when he ran in high school, when he was trim and in good shape. He watched the screen and saw Michael Johnson shooting ahead.

Joe Sims *was* Johnson, running effortlessly, in perfect physical condition, his mind clear, confident in his abilities. And it was he, Joe Sims, running, breathing deeply in and out, sweating a healthy sweat, flying. The crowd was cheering him on. They were proud of him, all America was proud of him as he kept at it, plugging away, passing the others, leaving them in his dust, one foot after the other, left, right, left, right. He crossed the finish line first, broke his own record and won the gold medal. The crowd was on its feet, screaming, delirious with joy. They loved him. He could feel the love enveloping him. All America loved him. The whole world loved him. Because he was strong and courageous and most of all, determined. How good it felt. How good…

Dave Thomas, the CEO of Wendy's, spoke to him soothingly, homey-like, like an old friend. Someone you could trust. Good old Dave told him how delicious his product was and how much you got for your money. Sims could see how great it would taste. It made his mouth water. In his mind's eye – his mind's mouth? - he could feel his teeth sinking into it, as Dave's actually did, the juices soaking into his tongue and bathing his taste buds. He had just finished his Big Mac, and here he was, hungry again, looking at sly old Dave, that conceited son-of-a-bitch, grinning in that self-satisfied way, chomping away, smacking his lips, telling him to go out and get one of those whatever-you-call-them, just so the rich bastard could make even more money. Yeah, well, go screw yourself, Davey boy. Funny thing was that Sims knew he would have gone out and bought one or two of them if he weren't so damned comfortable in his easy-chair watching the Olympics and drinking beer.

If Janey were there, she would have gotten him something from the refrigerator. She would've had all kinds of good stuff in the fridge. He glanced at the pink teddy bear lying on the tray table. He loved Janey so much, damn her, but she had to go and get mad and run away. He hated her for leaving him, the bitch. *Just because he smacked her around a few times. Spoiled brat, it's her folks' fault; they babied her too much. I wish she were here, though.*

He tossed bottle number four to the floor and reached for the fifth. *The fifth is for…is for…* He unscrewed the cap, not noticing the pain as it cut deeper into his finger. *Shit, who cares what it's for.* He giggled and was surprised at the sound. *It's for making me feel good, that's all I need to know.* He took a long drink, then belched with satisfaction.

He frowned. He recognized that sappy music and knew the suckers were going to tell him that you needed to give your lady a goddamn diamond if you wanted to show her you loved her. The music sounded kind of classical and inspirational, the bastards, to make you think people who could buy diamonds were more cultured and made love in a more refined way than ordinary folks, like it was something sacred, for Chrissake. Well, okay, maybe it was sacred, but what the hell has that got to do with diamonds? Huh…! I bet if I gave Janey a diamond, she wouldn't have run off on me. But I just can't afford a diamond. No, I can't, damn it! He pounded his fist on the arm of the chair, raising a puff of dust. *Well, screw you, Mr. wise-ass DeBeers money bags. And you too, Janey, if what you needed was a diamond.*

The boxers were banging away at each other. *Go on, go on, go on, keep punching, Antonio, keep punching. I'm blasting away at the Cuban guy. He can't hurt me. I'm made of iron. His fists feel like friendly pats when he manages to land a punch, which he doesn't do too often, 'cause I'm fast on my feet, and I duck and weave. Jack be nimble, Jack be quick. But I'm punching the hell out of him. I'm creaming the bastard, creaming the Cuban, creaming my old man. What?! Creaming my boss, I mean that son-of-a-bitch Mr. Hanson. I'm knocking the shit out of him. I'm banging away, mashing him into a pulp.* For an instant, he saw Janey at the receiving end of his fists. Again. He pushed the image from his mind. It was Mr. Hanson. It was the Cuban champion. And the crowd was cheering. They were on their feet and screaming. *They love me. Yes, they love me. Yes they do. They really do.*

Tears streamed from Joe Sims' eyes. He was disturbed to find he was weeping. *What the hell am I crying about?* Mohammed Ali, feebly lighting the Olympic torch, flashed through his mind, followed by that scene of the people crowding around him, asking him for autographs. *Mohammed Ali was smiling, but he was in bad shape, couldn't speak, couldn't answer people's questions, could hardly move, it looked like. But he smiled. A dumb-looking smile. What the hell was the poor bastard smiling about?*

Joe was overcome by a sudden sadness. *A guy like that, the way he once was, and look at him now...*Joe began to sob. *Goddammit, what the hell do I give a damn about Mohammed Ali? He made his millions. He did all right. Why the hell do I give a damn?!* He sobbed even harder. He raised the fifth bottle to his lips, tossed back his head, closed his moist eyes and drained the bottle. Then he flung it to the floor. He felt a little better, calmer.

The women gymnasts were performing. *Women? They're tiny little girls, is what they are. And that giant of a coach – the Romanian guy – hugging the crap out of them, getting his jollies right in front of the cameras as if it was okay. Who's he kidding? But those tiny little girls sure have skill. And guts. Not afraid to get hurt. And they're cute. They have beautiful legs, too. Yeah, really beautiful. The Ukrainian one, with the name nobody can pronounce, the one that knows how to dance like a ballet dancer, she's even sprouting real live boobs. You could see them bounce. Boy, when they get a couple of years older...*

And perfect control over every damn muscle in their little bodies. They're so bouncy, so rubbery, so damned... What's the word? Flexible, yeah, that's it - and supple. That's what they are, supple. That's a good word. And the one from China, what a great smile to go with the legs, what a wonderful, bright smile. It makes you feel all warm inside to see her smile. She's smiling right at me, I can feel her eyes on me. Janey used to smile like that. Used to...back then...at me. But not lately. Just because of some lousy bruises once in a while. And a chipped tooth. That's no reason to run off and leave a guy, when a guy loves her like I do. Damn her to hell! I hate her! I'd like to kill the bitch!

Joe Sims registered what was taking place on the screen. There was that nice family - mother, father and little daughter - visiting Disney World. *Probably cost them a mint - the trip, the hotel, everything. And the kid looking so sad, so damned disappointed, after having dragged her mom and dad all through Disney World. What the hell does the little brat want, anyway? Oh, yeah. She looks up and her face brightens like the sun shining through the clouds. What does she see? Her dear old grandpa back in the land of the living? The face of God? Looks like she's having a religious experience. Oh, no! Jesus Christ, it's Mickey–freaking-Mouse!*

Then she whines in that sappy way that could make you puke, "I've been WAITING - my WHOLE LIFE - to meet YOU!" Then she runs over, the stupid little airhead, and hugs the goddamn asshole in a mouse suit like he was the dearest thing on Earth, her eyes closed the way Janey used to close her eyes when we kissed, to feel the kiss better.

Who the hell are they kidding? Mickey Mouse! She should be hugging her mom and dad, not that stupid son-of-a-bitch in a mouse suit. What kind of values are they teaching kids, damn it! What kind of family values? A little girl like that, pissed off at her folks after they spend all that money getting to Disney World, just because she hasn't seen her big-deal hero, Mouse Man. And then she goes all syrupy and weirdo when she sees him. She forgets about her folks and runs over to big-eared Mickey the Moron, who's nothing but a $5.25-an-hour jerk in a mouse suit, and then loves the hell out of him. The little bitch.

Damn, I could've had a nice little daughter like her, maybe, if Janey hadn't gone and made me so mad that time when I punched her in the gut and she couldn't catch her breath for a while. And then she bled and had to go to the hospital...

The tears streamed down his cheeks once more. His body shook. *That's when she lost the baby, and I know it was my fault. But she shouldn't have gotten me so pissed off! She shouldn't have. It was just a little punch, that's all it was. I didn't mean it.* He sobbed, took a deep breath and held it, then let it out.

He glanced at the pink teddy bear on the tray table, then reached for the sixth bottle and cursed when he saw it was the last one. He opened it by reaching across to hit the top against the window sill. Then he brought it to his mouth, head back, eyes closed and chugged it down. He wiped his mouth with the back of his hand, emitted a long series of belches and tried to focus on the screen, the screen that was hard to see because it was so misty. *Why does it look so misty?* Things looked out of focus and bent out of shape, as though they were under water.

The red-headed Italian with arms like Hercules was on the stationary rings – muscles bulging, body rigid, face blank, not showing any strain, l*ooking like it was a piece of cake, the conceited bastard.* Joe Sims was on the rings, felt his own iron muscles bulging, the deltoids, the biceps, the "lats," the "pecs" and the abs. He felt the power in his trim, hard body, every move perfect. The crowd went wild, they felt admiration for him, they felt love. They all loved him. Janey would be sorry, now. But wait. He saw Janey among the cheering crowd. No, she wasn't cheering, she just stood there quietly. On her face was a look of admiration, of pride, of awe, of love. Then she slowly glided down out of the stands, strode across the field, passed in slow motion through the delirious throng and came up to him. She looked adoringly into his eyes. Then she held out her arms...

∞ ∞ ∞

Joe Sims awoke at 6:30 A.M. to Ann Curry on NBC News. She was talking about the TWA explosion, showing color footage. Then she reported the latest news on the bomb at the Atlanta Olympics. She even managed to look concerned, *like it really mattered to her, the phony. Death and destruction...every day, every miserable goddamn day. That's all there is. What the hell's it all about?*

Ann Curry told him it was 6:40. Christ! Time to get my ass in gear for my shift at the ice cream factory, where it's a hundred damn degrees all day long, even though I'm grabbing cold ice pops and sticking them into boxes, one after the other, after the other, after the other, hour after hour, day after day...

He was in his tattered and stained easy-chair, still wearing yesterday's clothes, reeking of sweat, sour ice cream and stale beer. And the taste of shit in his cottony mouth (get the blue mouthwash) and a sledgehammer bashing in his skull (grab the Aleve). He looked down and saw the empty bottles littering the floor. *Janey would have gotten rid of them, cleaned up.* Then he noticed he was clutching the pink teddy bear to his heart, the one he had bought when Janey told him she was pregnant. And he felt, along with his dry mouth and his aching head, the sensation of falling down an elevator shaft straight to hell.

"Oh, Momma, Momma...!" he whimpered aloud. "What's happening to me?"

Muscles stiff and cramped, he forced himself to get up out of the chair. With great effort, he lurched toward the bathroom. He pushed himself. He would make it to work on time. He could do it. Yes, he could. He would. He'd make the 400 meters and come in first, because he was a winner, a champion. He'd be awarded the gold medal. Everybody would cheer for him. And would admire him. And would love him. Yes, love him. Even Janey. He'd just keep running and running and running...

∞ ∞ ∞

Joe Sims kept running along the tree-lined sidewalks past the single-family dwellings where he knew happy families lived, couples with children who rode tricycles and boarded the school bus every morning, pushing and shoving, making a cheerful racket. He was running against the clock. He had to get to work on time. He hardly noticed the leaves that were starting to turn from green to pale yellow and red. He hadn't even had time to pack a bologna sandwich for lunch. He'd make do with the ice cream employees were allowed to eat on the job.

He heard the train whistle as he walked toward the tracks he would have to cross on his way to the Lakeland Ice Cream Factory. The factory, two blocks past the rails, loomed before him in all its dirty grayish-yellow bleakness. Looking at the windowless mass made him queasy. And he was out of shape, he acknowledged. He was no longer running as fast as when he left the house. He was no Michael Johnson. He was panting, sweating, slowing down. His heart was pounding, his temples throbbing.

He turned his head to the left. The train was in sight, gleaming in the sun. It came from far-off places. It was going to far-off places - places he had never seen - never *would* see. It was shiny, beautiful, as it sped smoothly along the tracks, free as the birds overhead. The birds didn't have to work. All they did was eat all day long. Their food was everywhere, free for the taking. They didn't have a boss, didn't have a care in the world.

He looked ahead and saw the factory, felt the factory as a blow to his stomach, as a weight on his chest. He could already feel the hellish heat, see Mr. Hanson's pink face and hear his grating voice calling him a lazy bastard. Joe Sims felt sick. His stomach was twisting into a ball. His breaths came in gulps. His pace slowed further. He felt as though he were running in a dream, his legs weighing a hundred pounds each, moving in slow motion.

He was almost at the tracks. The silvery locomotive with the red stripe gleaming brightly, reflected the morning sunlight. It was cheerfully blowing its whistle in greeting, which made Sims feel better, almost happy. He reached the rails and paused to catch his breath. He stood on the crossties, panting, and looked at the factory with dread. He shivered from cold sweat as a light autumn breeze stroked his shirt.

He felt an invisible wall beyond the rails, a force-field emanating from the factory, a presence that would not let him pass. Joe Sims turned to face the beautiful train that merrily whistled as it rushed to meet him. He could see right through the locomotive into the passenger cars, into the car where Janey sat with their daughter, the one who loved Mickey Mouse. They forgave him. They were smiling at him. They would pick him up on the way to Disney World. He opened his arms wide to receive them.

THE UNEXAMINED LIFE

Having learned nothing from a fruitless but expensive telephone call to the London headquarters of the British Philosophical Society, I decided to take a chance and make arrangements to fly to London. I felt that the best attitude to adopt was to assume that the Society had indeed accepted my paper. Why wouldn't they, based on the abstract I had sent them? I definitely would be participating in the Second International Colloquium on George Berkeley.

My intuition was correct, as usual. I was scheduled to speak on August 29 at 11:30 A.M. There were Berkeley scholars from all over the world, many of whom I knew. That is to say that I knew them by name and reputation. Most were American and British, but there was a sprinkling from other countries as well. There were delegates from Australia, Canada, New Zealand, Holland, Denmark and Sweden. There were even a few from Poland and Japan. In fact, there was this South American at the Colloquium – a South American, of all things! I don't remember precisely from what country, but what's the difference? It doesn't really matter. Furthermore, this South American was not even a Berkeley scholar. I hadn't ever seen his name in any of the philosophy journals; he was nothing more than a fiction writer. Can you believe it? This novelist, or short-story writer, or whatever he was, coming from some remote region of the southern hemisphere, was scheduled to speak during the same time slot I was. Poor devil! Who would be fool enough to attend the paper given by this South American upstart who wasn't even a professor of philosophy, to boot? A pathetic spectacle is what it was going to be, I thought. After all, I had published more than 15 articles on philosophy in learned journals, six of them specifically on Berkeley.

Moreover, they told me that this fiction writer had published nothing of importance on Berkeley, nor even on philosophy in general. He wasn't a specialist in philosophy. How did he have the nerve? And a South American, no less. Oh...have I already mentioned that?

I was thinking that he probably spoke English like some illegal immigrant, and, to top it all off, they said he was blind. Blind! Can you imagine? I wondered if he was going to give his speech by heart, since, obviously he couldn't use any notes. Impossible. What a pitiful spectacle it was going to be!

The lecture hall I was assigned was able to accommodate about a hundred persons. I noticed that, during the first day's sessions, there were always at least 50 people present in that room, eagerly listening and taking notes. Since I was scheduled to speak at the same time as the blind South American, I figured there would be a pretty sparse audience - pitifully sparse - for his talk. For obvious reasons, most of the participants would naturally attend my talk. There would be one problem only, I thought: the public wouldn't be able to fit into the lecture hall, and part of the dense crowd would be inconvenienced by having to remain standing close to the doors in order to hear me.

On that first day of the conference, I went to hear Yoko Hitachi's talk. Yoko was a very attractive Japanese woman of 28 or 29 years of age, whom I had met at the welcoming banquet. Being a bachelor (I never found the time for having a family. My career is my family.), I thought that perhaps Yoko and I could…well, you know what I mean. After all, I'm only 45 years old, a distinguished, intelligent, intellectual, not bad-looking, eligible bachelor. And she was very attractive and charming. Furthermore, I'm sure you know that Japanese women are trained from childhood to please men.

At any rate, I attended her lecture, even though I really would have preferred to hear Lance Buttwell, the renowned Berkeley scholar from Oxford. But what the hell… Most of the participants must have flocked to Buttwell's talk, since the hall in which Yoko presented her paper contained no more than ten people. To tell the truth, I was surprised to find even ten persons there; after all, when Buttwell speaks…I would have to suppose that those who attended Yoko's talk weren't aware of Buttwell's importance. I was aware of it, of course, but I had my reasons for lending my solidarity to the young Berkeleyan from Osaka. Besides, the proceedings would be published later and I could always read Buttwell's paper at my leisure.

Actually, Yoko's paper was disappointing. All she spoke about was the problem of translating Berkeley into Japanese. And her pronunciation of the English language was an atrocity, an attack on the heritage of Shakespeare. Our noble language was dealt a blow the violence of which was comparable only to that perfidious attack on Pearl Harbor on that day of infamy, December 7th!

Oh, well, no use allowing myself to be carried away. But her English was a travesty, believe me. Let me give you an example: the title alone, of her paper, sounded like, "Puroberems of Turansurating Berukery furom Engurish into Japanezu." Can you imagine? But it paid off: my attending her talk, that is.

Those other clods - and I'm positive that most of them were married men, although it's beyond me how a true Berkeley scholar can have any time for wife and family – those clods were all vying for her attention. Can't blame them, really. She was, after all, beautiful, young and Japanese. And Japanese women are trained from childhood to please men. You know that, don't you? At any rate, I persuaded her to have dinner with me the evening of her talk. I was glad I had foregone Buttwell's paper and had gone to hear hers instead. "Cast your bread upon the waters..."

The conversation was sparkling during dinner. I had her entire attention. I could tell that I was making a highly-favorable impression on her. And, why not? With my knowledge of Berkeley's life, my insight into his philosophy, my *savoir faire*… She was definitely impressed. She didn't say very much about Berkeley; after all, she was young, she had no professional experience (that was her first paper) and, after all, she *was* from Japan. And well, you know, Japanese women are trained...

She told me about Japanese customs, the Japanese countryside, Mount Fuji, the fishing villages...and her idiosyncratic pronunciation of English was growing on me. It was kind of...charming.

After dinner, I cunningly mentioned to her that there was this fascinating program on television about the European Common Market that I was dying to see, but that I had been having difficulty getting that particular channel on the T.V. set in my room. I thought she would invite me to her room to watch it, and, well...you know what a sly devil I am. However, the poor creature didn't get my drift. I was too subtle for her, I suppose. She covered her mouth with her hand, giggled - you know how Japanese women are - and advised me to complain to the management.

Well, no use rushing things.

Yoko and I had breakfast together the following morning, or, rather, Yoko, I and Lance Buttwell. What irony! I hadn't attended Buttwell's talk - something he could not have noticed, since there were over a hundred people present in the hall - and yet, there I was, having breakfast with the famous Buttwell. I happened to run into them as we approached the hotel coffee shop, you see. I'm sure he must have read several articles of mine, although he was too diplomatic to bring them into the conversation in Yoko's presence. After all, she had not yet published and he wouldn't have wanted to embarrass her.

Unfortunately, I didn't see Buttwell at lunch that day. I would have liked to cultivate his friendship more fully. I didn't see Yoko either. I imagine she must have gone shopping; you know how Japanese women are. Consequently, I stayed at the hotel for lunch, as did most of the conference participants. As it turned out, I was seated with several of the most boring people you could possibly imagine. "Crashing bores," as our British cousins say. Gilbert Cox was at my table. He insisted on being called *Gib* or *Coxey*, no doubt to show he was down to earth, a *regular guy*. You know, a sort of reverse snobbery. I forced myself to address him as *Gib*; I didn't think I could quite handle *Coxey*. He's with some absolutely insignificant four-year college out in South Dakota, or North Dakota, or Nebraska or some wretched place stuck out on the prairie, for heaven's sake.

Then there was this Morris Silverberg, or Silverstein, or Silverman, or something equally redolent of that particular ethnicity, if you take my meaning, who teaches at City College of New York – *naturally* - and is really much more interested in the Talmud than in Berkeley. Well, after all, what could you expect? Guess who else was at my table? You guessed it: that blind South American. Can you imagine? What a motley crew! Well, this South American spoke English much better than I had expected, after all, though not perfectly. He had some kind of weird accent, something between Irish and Spanish, if you can imagine such a thing. And he knew something about Berkeley, too. I was surprised because I'm not often wrong in my first impressions about people, as you know. He was more interested in fiction writers and poets, like Edgar Allen Poe and Samuel Taylor Coleridge and some other writers who are really quite *passé*. I'd never even heard of some of them, like Wilkie Collins, I believe, and some such Chesterfield or Chesterville or Chesterton, if I recall correctly. He prattled on and on - I thought he'd never stop - about writers no one ever heard of, South American writers with those weird, impossible-to-pronounce names, names that are - I'm sorry - impossible to remember. Names that sounded, for heaven's sake, like the kind our illegal aliens have. Can you imagine?

Well, back to the main issue. I finally presented my paper, at the same time as that South American fiction writer. Afterward, I was told - you're not going to believe this - that so many people flocked to his talk that there weren't enough seats, that they were filling the corridor outside the lecture hall, near the doors. And, by the way, the fact that some people actually told me this, that they rubbed my nose in it, so to speak, shows a deplorable lack of sensibility, of common decency, don't you think?

And, I swear, even though you'll find it difficult to believe this, there were only three people in my section. *Three freaking people!!* Oh, I'm sorry. Please forgive my language, but it was such a disappointment! What a disgrace! I can't understand it. There must have been some confusion as to who was speaking in which room...

Then, to make matters worse, the moderator or chairperson of my section cut me off in the crudest manner imaginable, just as I was on the next-to-last page of my paper. He informed me, in a loud, disrespectful voice, that my time was up. I explained to him - and I had to interrupt my own paper to do this, of course, and in front of everyone (thank goodness there were only three people in the audience to witness my humiliation)- I explained to him that I had only one more page to read. But this coarse individual closed his eyes, as if to erase my presence, to dismiss me – in that abominably supercilious manner so typical of the Brits - and merely repeated that my time was up. He even had the effrontery to add that he wanted to hear at least the end of that South American fellow's paper. Incredible, isn't it? The man looked like Nigel Bruce playing Dr. Watson, jowls and red nose and all. He stood up and said, in an annoyingly cheerful tone, "Too late. Terribly sorry, old chap. Ta."

Then he left, almost knocking me down in his haste. Well, you know how these Brits can be.

There was still time for the question-and-answer period, even though the moderator practically trampled me as he left on his way to the South American's talk. During this period, I couldn't help noticing that the three people in the audience were - it's painful to think about - the *maintenance* men, of all things, in overalls, with their brooms and mops and plungers and other tools. They were simply on their break and had sat down to rest for a while, nothing more. Still, one of them did take advantage of the question-and-answer session, and actually asked me a question. He said, idiotic Cockney accent and all, "Blimey, Gov', you must do quite a bit o' readin', then, don't you now?" My blood was boiling, but I limited myself to a dignified and laconic response. I said, "Yes, I do. Thank you."

And, do you know something? For days afterward, everyone was talking about the paper given by this South American with the unpronounceable name, which, on paper, looked more like a Danish or Swedish name than a Spanish or South American name. When it was pronounced, it was full of disgusting guttural sounds, except for the middle name, which was easy enough to pronounce, since it sounded something like *Louis or Louie*. And this Hispanic creature insisted we call him Georgey, even though his name is spelled J-O-R-G-E, which I know for a fact is pronounced Hor-hay in Spanish. Yes, that's right. Really patronizing, wasn't it? Did he think us incapable of pronouncing his name properly? What? Oh, yes. His last name is pronounced... Well, you spell it. B-O-R-G-E-S. Right, something like that. You've heard of him? Yes, that's right: Hor-hay Loo-ees Bor-hayz.

Be that as it may, I hadn't seen Yoko Hitachi for several days. I know this business with Yoko is something you find fascinating, so I'll get back to her. Buttwell told me that he had noticed her in the audience at Borges' talk. I was surprised that Buttwell would notice whether Yoko was or was not present, since, for some inexplicable reason, it was a completely chaotic mob scene at this blind fellow's talk. Maybe they all attended just to witness the novelty, the spectacle, of a man presenting a paper without being able to read it, who knew it by heart. It was a damned circus act! Can you imagine people who pride themselves on being intellectual having such vulgar taste?

At any rate, Yoko seemed to be having some difficulty finding me, so I was going to settle for having dinner with Buttwell on that last night in London. In this way, I could cement a friendship with him, strengthen our professional relationship. This could be helpful to me in my career. Unfortunately, he explained that he had just made other plans.

Later, I ran into Yoko and invited her to join me for dinner, but she said, and I quote verbatim: "So sorry. No have time now. I go to dining with very famous men. I go with Rance Buttwerr and Joruge Ruis Boruges." Then she added with that inscrutable, Oriental, diabolical smile, "You arriving too rate. No time now. So sorry."

She managed to hide her disappointment with that phony smile. You know how inscrutable these Orientals can be. What character, what strength of will. She really did a good job of hiding her chagrin. It was obvious that she would have preferred to have dinner with *me*, but she had already given her word. She realized she had missed the boat – if I may be permitted the metaphor. With all that shopping and all, she wasn't able to contact me for so many days. And now, as a matter of honor - you know how these Orientals are - she felt she was obliged to have dinner with Buttwell, a great Berkeley scholar, to be sure, but who is over 50 years old, is married and has two children about the same age as Yoko herself. And with some blind South American scribbler of no importance in the world of philosophy, and who, besides, looked like he was 80 or 90 years old, and I'm not exaggerating.

Furthermore, I suspect that, even in the world of fiction, of literature, this Hispanic fellow can't be any great shakes, either. He's never received the Nobel Prize, I hear, and people were of the opinion that he never would receive it. Now, at his age, after having written for so many years, never getting the Nobel Prize… Well, what the devil…if the Swedish Academy feels that way about him, he can't be too great. And now he's trying his luck at philosophy. Imagine!

Anyway, the three of them – Yoko, Buttwell and "Georgey" – must have really gotten drunk that last night, probably through boredom. They must have, because, on the following morning, when everyone was getting packed and preparing to go to the airport, I saw Yoko and Buttwell: pale, sleepy, dissipated-looking, as if they hadn't slept all night, or as if they had just gotten up, or as if they had not yet awakened! This, at 11 o'clock in the morning, getting out of the elevator, to have some breakfast, according to them. Can you imagine? Breakfast at 11 A.M., for heaven's sake. What a miserable evening they must have had to have gotten that drunk. Poor Yoko! Well, that's what happens when you don't plan your life carefully. "The unexamined life…," as Socrates said. Or was it Plato, or…? At any rate, she had her chance with me, but the conference was over.

She certainly screwed up.

NOSTALGIC JOURNEY

Sometimes, my friend, the mists of time begin to part, allowing partial views of past events to come to mind with what seems to be a luminous clarity. If the events in question affected one in a most personal way, a most intimate way, the recollection of them tends to be suffused with an aura that is commonly referred to – erroneously of course – as "romantic." At times, the experience, in retrospect, appears to have been so pleasant, so stimulating, so satisfying, that one is tempted to relive it. Of course, the danger in attempting to do this is not taking into account the fact that history does not repeat itself, not really, especially if that experience took place when one was young and is now old. I was aware of this, of course, but the memory of our honeymoon, and of the city in which we spent it, was so extraordinarily gratifying, that my wife and I decided to return.

In a town of Western Europe, whose name I do not wish to recall, to paraphrase Cervantes, the events I am about to relate took place. We hadn't been there since our honeymoon, 40 years earlier, but we retained pleasant memories of its clean streets, friendly citizens, first-class restaurants, good theaters and, of course, the famous Opera House. We had looked forward to our return for many years, and finally found ourselves in that enchanted city once more. We were going to see a production of "Countess von Sacher-Masoch," you know, the supposed wife of the novelist for whom Masochism is named. More about this later.

When we arrived on a Sunday, we decided to have dinner in an elegant restaurant. The city seemed eerily deserted, except for the disreputable characters hawking drugs in every alley, and prostitutes on every street corner. Most objectionable about them was that they were not very attractive, I might add. To say the least, I think that they should have had to pay the men, rather than the other way around. At least if they were good-looking…

But, as it happened, they detracted from whatever beauty the city had. I suppose if one is desperate…ah, but to be fair, I must concede that there was one who wasn't bad. No, not bad at all. She stands out in my mind because, at the very moment I noticed her, I injured my knee against a lamppost. Hmm? Oh, well, I wasn't watching where I was going and…well, I was intently observing a building across the street, you see, which was a magnificent example of Romanesque and Gothic architecture combined. Truly fascinating! My wife seemed angry at me, for some reason or other, but, after all, a tourist must be excused for looking at the scenery. After all, what were we there for?

There was not one policeman in sight. The city was filthy; excrement and urine, not excluding the human variety, were everywhere, along with uncollected - definitely ripe - garbage rotting in the sun. As you can imagine, a highly unpleasant odor permeated the entire city, clinging to our clothing, making it difficult to breathe. In other words, if you'll pardon my vulgarity, the whole town stank. It was utterly disgusting! It's hard to imagine why that pretty prostitute would choose to work in such a town.

Anyway, we had walked through all that filth for two hours without locating a single open restaurant, or even a hole-in-the-wall greasy spoon. Finally we had to settle for lunch in a bar. Now, when I say "bar," I refer, in this case, to a dimly-lit, long, narrow hall with a bar on one side. There were no tables; the room was too narrow for that. The cigarette smoke filled the narrow chamber, along with some other kind of sickly-sweet fumes that I was unable to identify. Actually, I'm not sure which was preferable: the noxious atmosphere in this den of iniquity or the stench hovering over the city out-of-doors.

Some of the patrons of this sinister lair – faces hard and hawk-like – stared unwaveringly at us. The other denizens simply gazed, expressionless, into space, as though they were in a hypnotic trance or a state of catatonia - or even in a state of religious ecstasy.

And when I say "lunch," I mean stale white bread enclosing some sort of unidentifiable material, or perhaps "matter" would be more accurate. We were able to choose among brown, yellow or green contents. When I asked the bartender, who I believe was an immigrant from somewhere in southern Asia, about the contents of the sandwiches, he smiled and said, "Oh, there is great variety, indeed, sir. To wit: brown matter, yellow matter or green matter. All very fine victuals, indeed, sir!" He smiled, I believe, somewhat too broadly. When I asked about the exact contents of that tricolor selection of sandwiches, he said, "Ah, my dear sir, these are secret recipes. Our chef is most jealous of his secrets and shares them with no one, not even with his wife, nor with me." And I'm quite sure the scoundrel winked at someone at the bar. I suspected I heard someone chortle, though he might have just been clearing his throat. At least that's what I wanted to believe.

By this time we were somewhat nauseated by the stench of the city and by the noxious atmosphere in this bar, yet we were desperately in need of sustenance. We reluctantly, yet determinedly, chose the yellow sandwiches. That color, it seemed to us at the time, contained fewer possibilities for material of dubious provenance. The bartender unctuously assured us that we had made an excellent choice, and presented the sandwiches with a flourish worthy of the sommelier at a fine French restaurant presenting a bottle of Chateau Neuf du Pape. Once more, I thought I heard someone clearing his throat.

The sandwiches had an odd flavor, not one we could actually identify, but, as I said, we were starving, becoming somewhat weak with hunger. After we finished our elegant repast…all right, I'll try to present the facts without sarcasm. When we finished our disgusting mystery sandwiches, as there was still time to kill before the play would begin, we went to visit the famous cathedral.

Something occurred there that you will find impossible to believe. While we strolled through the deserted cathedral, I noticed a man following us and placing benches and barricades behind us as we proceeded. It was as though he were cutting off our escape route. He turned out to be the sexton whom I had asked if we could visit the frescoes in the nave. Yelling at us like a deranged person and as though he were at a great distance from us, he bellowed, "Hey! Don't you know what a presbytery is?"

I must admit that I did not know what the word *presbytery* meant, but who was this man to be interrogating me, and in such a rude manner? I responded somewhat ill-humoredly, I must confess. I indignantly asked, "Are you testing me? Is this some sort of quiz?"

He bristled at my response. His thin face, behind gold-rimmed spectacles, reddened. He practically spat out the words,   "Maybe you need to go back to grade school and learn something, you ignoramus!"

I don't know how I allowed myself to become so enraged, but I found myself raising my fist in front of his weasel-like face. The demented sexton went pale, turned on his heel and bolted, taking refuge in the sacristy while continuing to inveigh shrilly against me from there. I, vociferating just as loudly as he, but adding a manual signal as well, urged him to, shall we say, have amorous relations with himself, if you know what I mean. My wife was mortified.

I would never have believed that something like that could take place in a church, of all places. And believe me, what I've just related is making a long story short. I've provided only the bare bones of this inglorious encounter. I must admit, I lost my temper, but the high expectations we had on entering the city, dashed by the experience of walking through that stinking cesspool, then eating who-knows-what in that sinister den of iniquity, followed by seeking solace in the peace and quiet of a majestic cathedral, looking forward to seeing exquisite artwork, only to be accosted by this madman...well, you can imagine. Incidentally, we suffered from severe stomach cramps that night, plus two days of running to the bathroom and gorging on Immodium pills. Hmmm... Perhaps the degree to which the gastronomic arts had deteriorated in that once epicurean city would explain the feces-strewn streets and the concomitant sulfurous odor that clung to the very walls like a leech to its host. But that's neither here nor there...

Be that as it may, having left the church, we headed directly for the theater. The drug dealers were still plying their wares, as were the unsightly whores. Still and all, I remember that attractive one we had seen earlier. Beauty among the beasts. Hmm... But I transgress...er, I mean, digress...

At any rate, as we approached within two blocks of the theater, we saw this man sporting a Sherlock Holmes cap - I believe it's called a deer stalker cap. I am not joking! And he wore the same kind of cape I've seen Basil Rathbone wear in the role of the archetypal sleuth in those wonderful films of the '40s. I'm not exaggerating! He rapidly scurried along the street, as though he were being chased by assassins. Hmm...come to think of it, perhaps he was. After all, the way that city is these days. Besides, we found out later that he was a theater critic. In that case, assassins would not be out of the question - only fitting, at times.

At this point, my wife and I, observing this eccentric person, were seized by such a fit of laughter that tears came to our eyes. This was the brightest moment of our miserable day. We were laughing hysterically when we arrived at the theater to see "Countess von Sacher-Masoch," a good title for the experience we were about to undergo. The play turned out to be an excruciatingly insipid drama from the 1950s, filled with clichés, in which the refrain was always the same: pleasure is concealed in pain, and pain is concealed in pleasure – the kind of trash you'd expect from a high school playwright, a rather unimaginative high school dramatist with too many courses in self-esteem under his or her belt, I might add. And the acting...the actors would make Arnold Schwartzenegger and Sylvester Stallone seem like Sarah Bernhardt or Sir Lawrence Olivier, by comparison.

Ah, but there was one actress who stood out – no, not because of her acting ability. Good heavens, no, far from it! But she was quite beautiful, gorgeous, actually. She had a very small part. Never even said more than five words, and those five words she recited as though reading off the winning lottery numbers. But she looked the spitting image of that young prostitute I had seen earlier. Yes, yes, that's right, when I hurt my knee on the lamppost. In fact, I suspect she might actually have been one and the same person. Conditions being what they are in that economy, one has to have more than one job to stay afloat.

Getting back to the play. People in the audience were yawning and anxiously, tormentedly, imploringly, asking each other how many acts there were in this wretched production. Unfortunately, there were three. My wife and I were too polite to leave before the end, although half the audience had done just that. Finally, this ghastly play came to its inglorious conclusion. Some remaining members of the audience applauded with that slow, deliberate, ironic clapping that is actually worse mockery than booing and hissing. The theater critic cum faux detective was one of these masters of sarcasm.

The actors dutifully appeared on stage, holding hands in solidarity - or perhaps for safety - and bowed deeply to the remaining members of the audience, who, by this time, were skulking toward the exits like Napoleon's army in its retreat from Moscow.

However, filled with rage by the crowd's rudeness, the leading man angrily made an obscene gesture involving one hand chopping into the folded inner elbow of the other arm. The pretty actress, emboldened by this display, brandished her uplifted middle finger and silently mouthed an obscenity I refuse to repeat. Their courage originated in believing that everyone's back was turned to them and, therefore, could not see their actions.

It's amazing, when you think of it, how expressing oneself, even though you believe no one is receiving the message, brings a certain relief. It's like writing a scathing letter to someone you abhor and then destroying it. Of course, I had turned my head to see if the cast was still bowing, especially the pretty one, and, for my pains, was rewarded with the sight of these gestures. I thought the actors should have considered themselves lucky that the audience did not rise halfway through the play and make similar gestures to *them*. If not worse, such as screaming insults and obscenities at them, or, more expressively, exiting to gather some of the uncollected garbage and other ordure, and then returning and launching these fetid missiles at the actors.

Sorry, my imagination is getting the better of me. I do feel sorry for the breathtakingly pretty young thing who had to make ends meet - no pun intended - by engaging in such a demeaning profession, renting her lovely body to strangers. But, even more shameful, more worthy of contempt, was her taking part in that abominable play.

To get back to the actual events...we finally departed from that theater of the absurd, once more preceded by the theater critic disguised as Sherlock Holmes. He was in even more of a hurry leaving the theater than he was arriving. In his febrile haste, he shoved aside several elderly women, knocked to the filthily sticky floor two children, and even trampled on two canines (yes, they are allowed on the premises) whose piercing yelps went through me like fingernails scraped against a blackboard. Undoubtedly, he couldn't wait to escape the scene of that travesty.

He would probably begin to write a caustic review of the play as soon as he raced across his threshold, without even taking the time to remove his idiotic costume. This is what I assumed, at any rate. However, once on the street, I noticed that he was actually hurrying to join a group of men of all ages who were lining up around the corner by the stage door. I saw him extract his wallet from his breast pocket, and then feverishly count the bills. I can't imagine why.

Appalled, dismayed and horrified by our unspeakable experience in that once-noble city, we got into our rented car and fled, like the souls of the damned escaping from the bowels of hell. We had spent ten hours in that stinking theater of the absurd. And by "theater of the absurd," I refer, of course, not merely to the theater, but to the city itself in all its ignoble entirety. The entire episode sullied the memories we had of that formerly-proud city, and cast a pall over the intimacies we shared during our honeymoon. It was as though someone had splattered manure against a beautiful and treasured painting. Well, as the Roman said, "Sic transit gloria mundi."

No, you fool, it does not mean "Gloria felt sick on Monday on the subway."

But I've learned a lesson: it is better to live on nostalgia, on one's memories, than to revisit the scene of past glory.